THE MYSTERIOUS CALL

NAMIT SHASTRY

ISBN 979-8-89133-901-9

CONTENTS

PREFACE

This book, 'The Mysterious Call', is my first stab at writing, especially in a genre where many classics already shine like the Pole Star. My humble attempt is my way of expressing gratitude to those great authors and thought leaders whom I aspire to become one day.

I hope the readers will bestow their attention upon this work, and that the narration, plot, and prose will keep them hooked. The story is set in the early 1980s in London City, where Senior Police Inspector Richard Carlsen receives a call, be it true or a prank, which leads him to a bungalow.

Bungalow Number 9 is shrouded in secrets, and each time Richard attempts to solve a piece of the puzzle, he finds himself mired deeper and deeper in mysteries. The characters, oddities, and settings change at the drop of a hat, keeping Richard on tenterhooks. Each character Richard encounters during his investigation has a different story to tell, whether it be a lie or the truth, Richard must discern.

Discover how Richard escapes the web of lies and solves the most intricate puzzle, albeit at the cost of a horrendous personal loss.

I believe that the gripping storytelling will compel readers to turn page after page as the suspense and thrill unfurl. I trust that this work will not disappoint and will be well worth your time and attention.

ACKNOWLEDGEMENTS

I would like to express my gratitude to Notion Press, my publisher, who has supported me at every step, and to my school, GIIS Noida, for providing me with this wonderful opportunity. I couldn't thank them enough for helping me discover the writer within me. I could never have imagined that I could write a fifty-thousand-word story.

I must extend my thanks to Dr. Nisha Shastry, an accomplished writer, who inspired me to translate my story and plot into words, assuring me not to fret over the narration and prose. She always emphasises that a sincere effort, made with wholehearted dedication, will resonate with those for whom it is intended.

Last, but certainly not least, I want to express my appreciation to my grandparents – Nana, Nani, and Dadi – for always being there for me, as well as to my mischievous little brother, Keshav.

MAIN CHARACTERS

1. **Richard Carlsen**– Senior – Inspector, London Police
2. **Emily Carlsen** – Richard's wife
3. **Vijay** – Manager, Allen Manufacturers
4. **Nicholas** – The Attacker
5. **Louis** – Sub – Inspector, London Police
6. **Watson Taylor**– Head constable, London Police
7. **John** – London Port Manager
8. **David** – Crewman
9. **Alex** – Sub-Inspector who accompanied Richard
10. **Forbes** –Commissioner, London Police
11. **Johnson Allen** – Salt company owner and owner of Bungalow no. 9
12. **Robert** – Lab in-charge
13. **Andrew** – Carlson Marine & Transport Co., boat company
14. **Henry Walter** – Mafia lord of Drug Suppliers
15. **Sam Ross** – Mafia lord of Arm Suppliers
16. **Dominic Kirk** – Former known drug dealer
17. **Wordsworth** – Richard's friend, corporate field expert
18. **Ms. Taylor** – Watson's Wife
19. **Sarah Walter** – Henry Walter's daughter

20. **Marianna** – Sketch Artist
21. **Lisa Ross** – Sam Ross's Daughter
22. **Melvin** – Constable, London Police
23. **Dr. Johnathon** – Expert in narcotics
24. **Others** – Craig Smith, Alexander, Stewart, Godfrey, Halliday, Asst. Registrar etc.

Time Check

Phone call	12 MIDNIGHT	06-10-1982 Wednesday
Reaching Bungalow no. 10	12.45 AM	
The Gruesome Murders	2.00 AM	
Forbes Call	4.45 AM	
Richard at London Port	7.00 AM	
Forbes Call – the second time in a short while	10.00 AM	
Richard back to London Port	12 NOON	
Getting in Cigarette Boat	2.00 PM	
Reaching Harwich	4.30 PM	
Return from Harwich	8.00 PM	
Attack by Nicholas	8.30 PM	
Nicholas in Hospital	9.00 PM	
Sketch by Marianna	10.00 PM	
Return home	12 midnight	07-10-1982 Thursday
Meeting Robert	8.30 AM	
Meeting Asst. Registrar - HM Land Registry office, Croydon	10.00 AM	
Meeting Wordsworth	12 noon	
Meeting Dominik Kirk	1.30 PM	
Leaving for Grangemouth	10:00 PM	

Reaching Grangemouth	6:00 AM	08-10-1982 Friday
Encounter with Andrew Carlson	7:00 AM	
Meeting with Vijay	8:00 AM	
Meeting Sarah Walter	11:00 AM	
Leaving back for London	1:00 PM	
Reaching London	9:00 PM	
Meeting Nicholas in hospital	9:00 AM	09-10-1982 Saturday
Meeting Forbes	10.30 AM	
Meeting Robert	11.30 AM	
Basement discovered	1:00 PM	
Arrest of Ms. Taylor	2:00 PM	
Leaving for Polwarth	4:00 PM	
Reaching Polwarth	12 midnight	
Meeting Craig Smith (knowing about Alexander and Stewart)	12.30 AM	10-10-1982 Sunday
Catching Vijay	2.00 AM	
Adventure at the Allen Manufacturing Factory - Scotland	6.00 AM	
Back to London	4.00 PM	
The Last fight	6.00 PM	

From the Diary of Richard Carlsen - 1982

Chapter I

THE CALL

The ligneous desk on which I had my hands was unoccupied. Neither the books could make their way onto it, nor could the files. It was only a Union Jack flag which stood on the desk.

I was a tall, fair, well-built man, blessed with thick silky hair and bluish eyes that could mesmerise visitors to the Baker Street police station by my looks. Many female complainants would visit our police station just to catch a glimpse of me or strike up a conversation with me to spend a little time with me. I was a popular guy in my mid-thirties with a stout build to go with my charming face.

After the long and tiring days and nights of a complex investigation, I was sitting in my cabin with my legs on a hassock, gifted by a dentist friend.

My usual pastime was reading and re-reading classics such as 'The Sign of Four', and I was so engrossed in the plot that I felt as if I were the protagonist Sherlock Holmes. The pendulum clock hanging majestically in the police station's large office space was about to witness its two hands imbricate each other, and the midnight bell was about to disturb me. However, if something rang at that hour, it was the clangorous ring of an unwanted telephone call. The suspense of the classic 'Sign of Four' was about to unfold when my attention was brutally distracted by that clangour.

I hoped that any of my team members would do the honours, alas, none of them were active and effervescent at that hour, to tear themselves away from their seats.

My team was filled with the most competent and professional officers and detectives; however, we had just solved a complex case that gave us almost a week of sleepless nights, and thus, they were sleeping like there was no tomorrow.

I tried to ignore that abominable sound and concentrate on the masterpiece created by Sir Doyle; however, the conscience inside me did not allow me to ignore it. Someone had knocked on the door of justice; the door of hope, and it was my abundant duty to answer.

With a sigh, I put the novel down and picked up the call, 'Hello, Baker Street Police Station, Senior Inspector Richard here.' I responded to the call in the most casual manner.

'A brutal crime is about to take place in Bungalow 9 in Notting Hill, Residential Area within half an hour.' The worried, painful yet melodious voice of a girl greeted me. She continued, 'Be here...' Suddenly, the phone hung up. Before the phone ended, I could make out a word which I overheard, 'You...' The tone of that 'You' was natural, still, I could sense the danger that she might be in; however, then I thought it could be a hoax. I waited to gather my thoughts and then went back to the world of suspense and mystery created by the master, Sir Arthur Conan Doyle.

I had just resumed when someone sat just beside me and took the novel away from my hand. It was my confidante – my partner in solving many cases and crimes – Watson Taylor. He was a Head Constable reporting to me; however, since our training days, we had struck a chord that made us the thickest of friends. Ever since our designations never came between our relationship.

'Who called at this hour?' Watson inquired while closing the novel and placing it neatly on my desk. Watson was a short man, with bare hairs forming a circular boundary on his bald head and a scar on his right hand. He was overweight, very overweight to be in my team of capable policemen. But his presence of mind at times got the better of the criminals. His sharpness defied his figure. He had helped me decode many mysteries that would have otherwise taken ages to fathom.

'What's the matter, Richard?' He yawned during the whole sentence, and this wasn't something new to me, for I had known him for a long time. He looked drowsy even at the most active hours.

I replied to him while relaxing in my chair and then standing, 'A girl tried pranking me. Some warning about a mishap that was going to take place.' I continued while walking toward the windowsill, 'Do I sound so foolish that anybody could get the better of me? Anyways, ignore it.' I started staring at the moonlight. The crescent moon looked magnificent. I was waiting for the usual whistling crescendo of the nightingales, which was absent that night. It was October, and it was foolish of me to expect the sweet songs that usually grace the summers. I took a cigar and smoked it for a while when Watson spoke.

'Richard, I think you understand we are sitting idle...'

'Idle. Not at all.' I gestured toward the closed novel on my desk.

Watson gave me an angry look. I looked outside the window and said, 'I am not indolent, Watson, but the city hardly rolls out the red carpet for a crime.'

'What's the harm if you address the matter? And don't forget you are Richard Carlsen – someone who could solve cases that the best of the officers refused to take.'

Watson's tone was quite persuasive, and he, to an extent, made me change my opinion. One of the sporadic occurrences where someone made me change my outlook. I was a man who stuck to his own opinions.

I stood up and put on my shoes and said to him, 'I don't know, Watson, what changed your thought process, but nowadays you look quite energetic to work, what a change.'

Then I peevishly added, 'I hope this lasts more than a few hours. Let's take ourselves to the other end of the call.'

Watson was happy. He put on his cap, took his baton and the car keys, and rushed out. I took my service pistol – the Smith & Wesson 10, and a few cartridges, and followed Watson.

While going out, I stopped at the cabin of one of the senior colleagues and said, 'Hey you...' I tapped the table on which my friend was resting his head and shoulders, and he seemed to be in a torpor.

The sub-inspector, a short man with a boring face but attractive features, just up from a nap, had mixed gestures on his face and looked at me as if I was the culprit disturbing his deep sleep. He got up from his seat, and before he could say anything, I said, 'I am heading for a case. Being the most senior at the place in my absence, hold the fort for a while.' He appeared to pay full attention, but his drowsiness seemed to get the better of him.

I made my way outside the station where Watson was waiting for me, standing near our official police car, a Vauxhall Astra. A small Astra protruded vaguely in the direction of the forward-facing side of the station and had a miniature boot and cramped seating space. The rear side of the car was not as bulging as in the previous models. It was not even shoulder-high. Looking at me, comparing my height, Watson said mockingly, 'A giraffe with a rabbit...'

'Can this giraffe drive the car now?' It was an astounding urge of mine because I didn't like driving cars, but today the nightingales didn't please me, and probably I wanted a change. The reason for my strange behaviour was unknown to me too.

'Ok.' He took the other side of the car, and we both entered it.

I closed the car's front door with a thud and turned the engine on with a slight swerve of the key. I pressed the accelerator, and the car started pacing forward, and I swivelled the steering.

I focused on my driving, as it had been a long time since I drove, but I was in touch. I found Watson intently focusing on the landscapes through the car window and allowing his fingers to enjoy combing his hair, which slithered on his cranium. Looking at Watson, I thought to strike up a conversation. In an interesting tone filled with enthusiasm, I started, 'Was the call a prank? What do you think?'

'Why do you say so?' Watson responded instantaneously.

'Don't know. Why would someone invite me for a crime that was about to take place?'

'Well, maybe something terribly wrong is going to happen.' Watson added with intent.

'Ok. Soon we will find out.' I said and swerved the handle towards the Notting Hill area.

'Well, where are we heading?' Watson inquired.

'Bungalow Number 9...' I said but couldn't complete it.

'Residential Area, Notting Hill,' Watson continued my words, in a tense tone while nervously swerving in his seat.

'Yes. How are you aware of it?' I questioned curiously.

'Well...' He took a lot of time to make a reply while I took another turn, and the Notting Hill Residential area was about to be reached.

'It's okay, Watson. Some things do make us hesitant,' I peevishly responded.

'I was not hesitating...' Watson responded in a terse tone, but he looked out of words.

'Don't be wretched,' I said.

He turned to my question as I put the car in top gear, 'I guess neither scream was heard nor any suspicious conversation could be overheard.'

'So, it may be a hoax,' I added.

'But anyone in London has guts to foul play, Richard Carlsen, that I doubt.'

'Maybe she was getting bored and wanted to look at a handsome face.'

'And in case she swoons looking at the gorgeous Carlsen, I am there to compensate,' Watson added.

We both laughed, and soon I swerved the car into the Notting Hill Residential Area.

I was staring at the movements that could be seen in the nearby bungalows. As we entered the area, I noticed a long marble gate that had the following words in bold: '*Residential Area*'. The guard who was supposed to be outside this gated community was sleeping, and the gates were ajar.

I saw someone highly drunk moving at a curve on the road. The area was a posh area, and its environs made it grander than the rest of the places in London; however, still, it seemed like a perfect place to commit crimes. Bungalows were separated by huge distances of 200 metres apiece; no one could come to know if something fishy was going on in one of the bungalows.

In no time, I zoomed past various bungalows, like numbers 25, 24, 23..., and we reached Bungalow No. 9, where our Vauxhall Astra had to stop at the boom barrier. The cabin nearby was lit, and the security guard there saw our vehicle. Unlike the guard at the main gate from where the Residential Area of Notting Hill begins, this security guard of Bungalow No. 9 was active and awake.

He waved his hand, and I rolled down the window. The guard, from the window of his security cabin, protruded outside and asked, 'Police, why are you here?'

His mannerisms were uncharacteristic of a security guard. Moreover, his language, appearance, looks, and dressing sense suggested that he was not from London but from some rustic town. He had a black furry jacket with a hoody and had covered his head. A short man with an unkempt beard, and it was clear that he was not well-versed in the duties of a security guard.

Watson thought to respond, sitting in the front passenger seat, shouting literally, 'Around twenty minutes ago, we received a call...'

I interrupted and completed his sentence, 'We received a call from the owner of this bungalow that there is some suspicious activity in the surroundings. He said that the security guard at the main gate also allowed anyone in and wanted police protection at this hour. So, we are here to inspect and see whether additional police protection should be given to this residential area.'

Watson was dumbfounded; it was rare for me to tell lies, but this was one such occasion.

The guard was perplexed, as he didn't expect the police at that hour. My tone was authoritative, too, and thus the poor guard had no choice. He was unclear whether the owner had called the police or not. He looked at me and Watson with intent as if asking some hidden questions. Nevertheless, he turned back picked up the intercom, and started dialling the number.

I could overhear the feeble sound of the ring that was coming from the receiver, which meant the security guard indeed had made the call. The call went unanswered, once, twice, and thrice. The guard was patiently dialling again and again.

In the meanwhile, I looked at the cabin where a police belt was hanging over the peg, and the black furry jacket the guard was wearing seemed expensive. I didn't think that even I could afford such expensive clothing.

I also noticed that while the guard was dialling the intercom, his middle finger had a bandage on. I, to lighten the mood, said, 'How did you hurt your finger?'

'I hurt it while cutting an apple,' he responded curtly while holding the receiver, waiting for an answer.

I was about to ask some more questions to that guard when Watson shouted, 'Allow us in.' Watson kept growling, 'You are interfering with the duties of a public servant.'

The guard seemed to be driven by the fear when he heard Watson's angry tone and the weird gestures my friend had put on display. Driven by that fear, the guard allowed the boom barrier to rise, making way for us, and I drove down the inner road that would lead us to the bungalow's gate.

The inner road was lined with branded cars parked alongside the bushes under some shade. The cars that enjoyed the shade were all branded and displayed the owner's success. They included the latest models of Mercedes, BMW, Rover 200, and more. The opulence was richly displayed.

We reached the main door, which was a large and sturdy rosewood door. We both got out of our Astra and stepped toward that rosewood door. I tapped the door. I kept on tapping but to no avail.

'I believe the bungalow is bereft of any occupant. A prank call indeed,' Watson summed up. His eyes looked concentrated on me, and I turned to his estimate. 'Probably,' but I continued knocking on the door.

'But why did the guard not tell us that the bungalow is unoccupied? Why was he trying with the intercom?' I questioned while continuing to knock on the door.

After many futile attempts, even thumping the door with my palms, an underwhelming feeling of belittlement shrouded me. I was about to leave the place with Watson when I saw something.

'Watson, Watson...' I exclaimed with childlike excitement. I continued, 'I saw some silhouette, and it seems some lamps are alight in the bungalow.'

'Well...' Watson took his time saying the only word, and this was all I could expect from him. It looked as if he wanted to continue but his intellect didn't entertain any words.

I whispered to Watson in a tone with a constant amplitude, 'Look for a surrogate entry as I will keep an eye here.' He had just crossed the gate with a few steps when a sound could be heard growing louder and louder. The sound seemed like a girl wearing high heels tapping on the ground, specifically on wooden flooring.

I put my hands together, producing a soft sound that was loud enough to make Watson turn around, and I gestured for him to stop and turn around as the gate opened with a squeaking sound. He then came back with his short legs making a gentle sound.

A tall lady with a dishevelled hairstyle, as if she had been in a fight, addressed us. She had a white hairband with a few black dots arranged in a different pattern. The hairband seemed of little use. Her face had a few scars, and blood was coming out from her finger. She was wearing a red top, which was torn near the wrist of the right hand. She had a heeled sandal, maybe the one that produced that clacking sound, while the other one was bare.

She had opened the gate just enough that I could catch sight of the messy study, a vase on the floor, a broken chair, and the dishevelled lady.

Curiously looking at me and Watson, and after a small pause, she peeped through the small space of the opened gate and asked, 'Hello officers. Have you received some complaint that marks your arrival?' Her tone varied with each word, and I couldn't be sure whether she was my caller. She looked afraid and exhausted from the recent events she had been a part of. She also seemed highly inebriated.

'Yes. The owner called us, suspecting some felony,' Watson intervened.

The lady uttered in a quaffed voice, 'Sorry, the owner is not here, and I don't think anyone called you from here.' This was an inexplicable response, and I did not anticipate it.

'We want to come in and check,' I said while taking a step closer and pressing the door gently to open it further up.

'Sorry, officer,' said the lady in a firm tone. 'Show a search warrant first.'

I was shocked. I thought the lady would be a victim and would help me enter the house. Instead, she was terse. The gate was slammed closed before I could entertain any further words. Watson was shaken by the kind of rudeness the lady displayed.

'Is the lady a victim herself?' I unequivocally questioned.

'I suggest you stay away from that, Holmes,' Watson responded while walking back toward our Astra.

'Well, I could smell brandy or maybe rum as she spoke. She was extremely drunk,' I said loudly to Watson.

The guard had also come in the meanwhile, and Watson looked at the guard and questioned, 'Is she the owner of this bungalow?'

'No, she's the owner's daughter,' the guard replied in a scared tone. His appearance and demeanour revealed that he was not very educated. His accent was unusual but good enough for me to understand him.

We headed towards the Astra car, and I whispered to Watson, 'I need to search this house as there is something fishy about the lady and the bungalow.' I continued, 'I will be back with a search warrant and some police force. In the meantime, you be on your guard and ensure no one escapes from this bungalow.'

'I don't think that much effort is required. We only met a drunk girl who might have created that mess.'

'Watson, something is telling me it is more than what meets the eye.'

'Okay, Richard,' Watson conceded.

'That's great,' I said. I started moving toward the gate.

'You are not going to the police station,' Watson said while watching me pass the Astra.

'Do you think we have time for that?' I retorted.

'No, we don't...'

I interjected before Watson could complete. 'I could observe a phone booth a few yards from here, and it would be of help.'

'Dialling the...?' Watson questioned while I paced away from him.

'Commissioner and then the sub-inspector, Louis,' I replied before Watson could complete his sentence.

'Is Louis of any use?' Watson said indifferently.

'He is a smart guy, but of late, his broken heart doesn't allow him to concentrate well.'

'Well, it was all Louis's fault...'

'Why are you digging for details?' I said over my shoulder while pacing away from Watson.

'I am not... Like I... Digging,' Watson hesitated while pronouncing his words, and I continued my stroll toward the phone booth.

Whether the girl was the same one who called me? The voice I heard was not inebriated, and it was extremely difficult to fathom whether the girl was the one who called. Why would she say a gruesome crime was going to be committed within half an hour? It was almost forty minutes since I had received that call. What kind of crime could have been committed? Was this a prank?

I was engrossed in my thoughts and didn't realise that I had reached the phone booth, which was around two hundred metres from Bungalow No. 9. The phone booth appeared dusty and seemed as if it was not used by people in the vicinity very often. The look suggested that it may not have been used for many months. I pulled the door, and it slowly opened, making a squeaking sound. I prayed that this phone booth would be operational. I didn't want to waste any more time.

I took the handset and dialled the numbers. I remembered the number of Mr. Forbes, my super-boss, the Commissioner of the London Police. He was our head and the most important member of the London police. We jovially called him 'the somnolent man' because he always appeared to have drowsy eyes.

The phone rang, and I thanked my stars. The ringing continued, and I waited patiently. I didn't know what was going on in that Bungalow, which appeared so mysterious. Something was telling me that some brutal crime was going to take place there. I needed to stop it. The phone went unanswered.

I tried again, and with each passing ring, my anxiety reached a new zenith. The phone went unanswered again. I was distraught, and I thought it would be better if I reached his house and woke him up. But that would take another hour and a half while I came back. I didn't know if I had that much time.

So, I tried the phone again. As the numbers I dialled connected me to Mr. Forbes, I was thinking about what I would say to him. It seemed that even my third attempt was going to be in vain. I thought of putting the headset back, and while I was putting it down, I heard a feeble voice,

'Hello...'

This gave me a fresh bout of energy, a feeling hard to express. The happiness was unbounded. I immediately said, 'Mr. Forbes, this is Richard.'

'Richard!!' shouted Mr. Forbes. 'Are you out of your mind?'

'I am really sorry to bother you at this hour,' I requested politely.

'What was the urgency? Why have you called me at this hour,' Forbes barked.

'I received a call around midnight, and some lady tipped me regarding a crime that was to take place in Bungalow 9 soon.'

'So, go immediately to Bungalow No. 9 and check. Why are you calling me?' Forbes was disdainful.

'I and Watson went there, but we met a girl who might be in her mid to late-twenties.'

'Richard, why are you telling me stories at this hour? Come to the point,' Forbes had now lost all patience. He would have slammed the phone down at any moment.

'The girl looked dishevelled, and the security guard looked suspicious. I saw that the house was in a messy state. I want a search warrant to search the house,' I concluded as fast as I could.

'Richard, are you as stupid as you sound?' Forbes shouted back.

'Sorry, did I miss something?'

'Missed something? You got a call, you went, you found some girl and nothing else. On such a small pretext, you want me to issue you a search warrant at this hour. Are you really that stupid? Go investigate it properly. If something concrete is discovered, come to the office tomorrow, we will think about the issuance of the warrant,' Forbes growled and slammed the phone down.

The conversation ended soon, but it left me in a lurch. What should I do now? I had no idea. Getting a warrant from that bulky bugger at this hour was stupid of me. I should have been more thoughtful.

Dejectedly, I opened the door of the small porta cabin converted into a phone booth. I stepped back and started strolling back, when it struck me. 'Louis. Yes, Louis it is. He could be of help.' I rushed back to the phone booth and immediately dialled another number.

I impatiently dialled the white-coloured numbers on the black circular disc slightly above the level of the keypad. Taking the handset to my ear, I sighed and waited for the call to connect. I looked at the ceiling of the booth and then came a voice, a heavy shrill voice followed by a giant yawning sound, 'Hello.' It was a low tone with which he started.

'Louis...'

'Mr. Carlsen.' His tone grew louder, and then his yawning oscitance vanished almost instantaneously.

'Take a few policemen, a forensic team, an ambulance, and lead the squad to Bungalow 9, The Residential Area, Notting Hill,' I hurriedly said.

'Any murder reported?' Louis questioned.

'No, but I suspect one.'

'You mentioned that no murder was reported, yet you want the full squad.'

'Yes.'

'Ambulance and the forensic...'

'I told you that I suspect one.'

'Any major reason that I deserve to know...'

'I received a call from some lady telling me that some brutal crime is going to happen in thirty minutes at Bungalow No. 9, Notting Hill Residential Area. I reached there and met a dishevelled girl in her mid to late-twenties. She had a cut on her finger, a messy room, bruises from slaps on her face, etc.'

'Was she the same girl who called you?' Louis questioned.

'I am not sure. She was highly drunk when she opened the door. After seeing me, she slammed the door in my face, tersely telling me to get a search warrant if I wanted to enter the house.'

'Understood. But that means she's not in trouble. Otherwise, who would refuse the help of Richard Carlsen.'

'I am not sure why she slammed the door in my face. I have a strong premonition that she is in trouble and some big crime is going to happen. I need help, and I need it fast.'

'I got the drift. Your directions will be followed.' He hung up the phone.

I felt a bit satisfied now. Though I knew that I didn't have a warrant, what I possessed was more important: the right to forceful ingress to the house. I believed a crime was about to be committed, and as the police inspector in-charge of the area, I had the authority to do what was in my power to prevent an offense.

I paced back towards the bungalow. I didn't realise that almost thirty minutes had been wasted in making these calls. Watson was alone, and he might need help. I ran towards the bungalow as fast as I could.

I reached the bungalow, and the security guard who had stopped us last time was not there. He might be inside with Watson, I thought. The boom barrier was still erect, and I ran inside the bungalow. In a couple of minutes, I was at the main door, which was now shut tight, and the bungalow was surrounded by complete darkness. The crescent moonlit bungalow looked ominous.

The Vauxhall Astra was there; however, I couldn't find Watson anywhere. The guard and Watson were both missing. I shouted, 'Watson...' and ran here and there but couldn't find any trace of Watson or the security guard. I took a full round of the bungalow and also went to the backside where a mini garden was maintained. Many colourful plants that, at a plain look, seemed like daffodils were there.

I took the full circle of the bungalow and came back to where I started, near my Vauxhall Astra. I screamed as loudly as possible, 'Watson.' He was too naïve to be missing at such an hour for an unknown reason. I was extremely worried about him now. I started pacing outside Bungalow No. 9 and soon I was on the main road. I rushed here and there, at times running as far as other bungalows, but to no avail. I couldn't find any trace of Watson.

Where had Watson gone at that hour? I was shocked. I dejectedly came back to Bunglow No. 9. I was tired and exhausted from the running and at the turn of the events. I saw that someone was sitting in the guard's cabin outside bungalow no. 9, and the boom barrier had been dropped down. I thought to check with the guard about Watson. I reached the security guard's cabin. 'Guard.' I was panting because of the sprint and said without looking at the guard. I slowly was gathering my breath.

The guard, upon seeing a police officer, came out of the cabin, when I had the occasion of looking at him. I got the shock of my life. He was a new person. This new guard was wearing a similar uniform to the earlier guard, but he was tall, reasonably well-built, and had a face covered with a beard and moustache. He wore expensive shoes. He looked more polished than the previous guard, but I doubted whether he was the real security guard or another impostor.

'Who are you?' I questioned suddenly.

'I am the guard of this bungalow,' he replied.

'Where is the other guard?' I asked.

'Which other guard? I am all alone here,' he responded plainly.

I was shocked. I replied, my face showing disbelief as if I had seen a ghost, 'I met another guard about thirty minutes ago.'

'That is not possible. I am all alone here. I went to answer the call of nature, and when I returned, I saw you running here and there, and then you came to my cabin.'

'My car is inside. Have you seen another police constable, Watson? He was here at the bungalow.'

'Sorry, Sir. I didn't realise that you had gone inside. But that is not allowed without a warrant.'

'What nonsense. I am looking for my friend,' I shouted.

'I am sorry,' the guard responded while blocking my way. He stood between me and the bungalow's outer entry.

'You can call the girl inside,' I said authoritatively.

'Which girl? The bungalow belongs to an old couple. There is no one inside,' the guard responded tersely.

'I just met a girl,' I shouted.

'I don't know what you are talking about,' the guard replied.

'I need to go inside, and that too now,' I growled.

'Sorry, I can't let that happen without a warrant,' the guard said.

I noticed that the guard was constantly looking at someone behind me as if trying to figure out what to say. I knew that something was fishy. Watson was missing, the girl was alone in that bungalow, she might be in trouble, and the bungalow was surrounded in complete darkness, while some time back, I had seen a small light coming from the bungalow.

I turned back immediately, and before I could notice anything, a strong light dazzled my vision. I spontaneously shouted, 'What was that?'

'Maybe some car,' the guard callously responded.

I understood that something was grossly wrong. This new guard was not letting me in. My investigative intuition hinted that I needed to enter the bungalow forcefully.

I gave the guard a hard stare. I had no option but to use my Smith & Wesson 10. I generally didn't like to use this option, but only in the most desperate times had I needed to. This was one such occasion. In no time, I took out my pistol and pointed it toward the guard. I shouted, 'You are letting me in, or you want to witness my ability with firearms...'

'Sir, I am just doing my duty,' the guard responded meekly. He was clearly frightened by my actions. He hadn't anticipated this.

'I know what duty,' I shouted back. Then I pointed my gun to signal him to remove the boom barrier and let me in.

The guard looked behind me and said, 'Sure.'

He then pressed the button, and the boom barrier was lifted. The guard gestured with his hands to walk in, and I put my pistol back in the holster. I walked inside, and the guard followed me. I knew that the guard was talking to someone, but who was that person? I needed to find that out.

I was slowly strolling towards the bungalow. The bungalow was large and sprawled across a huge landmass. I could see the various cars parked in front of the bungalow and a mini-garden behind it.

'Who are the owners of this bungalow? I inquired with the guard following me.

'An old couple. They used to live in this bungalow ever since my father served this post. I have succeeded him, and I am a loyal servant. The couple is unfortunately childless. Madam never wanted adoption, and so this bungalow lacks an heir. They don't live here anymore and visit rarely.' His description was detailed, and I noted the history. To this reply, I had a few moments of silence to offer.

I was dazed by his words. My brows furrowed, my eyes squinted, and a few wrinkles formed on my face. I repeated, 'Childless.' It was more of a rhetorical statement than a question.

It struck me – new guard, Watson missing, childless couple, a strange girl in the bungalow, a call warning about a crime to take place in the bungalow, old couple. These dots were flying around, but the thread to seamlessly connect them was missing. I had to find that thread.

I was so absorbed in these thoughts that for a moment, I lost track of my surroundings. I had a mental lapse where the realities around me ceased to exist. Suddenly, I stumbled, and the Havana Cigar Case that I carried in my shirt's right pocket fell to the ground. I wanted to look for it, but in the darkness, the crescent moonlight was insufficient to locate the case. I started looking around, bending down on my knees, but all in vain.

'Guard, do you have a torch?' I asked while still kneeling and searching the surroundings. My hands were moving left and right.

When there was no response for a few seconds, I shouted, 'Guard! Show the light!'

Still no response. I glanced up with a scowl on my face. To my surprise, there was no one with me. The person had slipped into the darkness. But how?

I sprinted towards the guard's cabin. I reached there, but to my surprise, there were none. I could see an engine revving up and a vehicle zooming past. I took out my S&W10, but the vehicle was far away, and it was beyond the reach of my bullets.

What could that vehicle be? My question was answered when I looked back at the various vehicles that were parked at that bungalow. BMW e21 was missing, and it meant the security guards were merely a cover. The culprit, after committing the crime, ran away in that car.

I was in two minds: whether I should go after this vehicle or whether I should go inside the bungalow. It was at that time that I heard a feeble sound, a yowl from the bungalow: 'Ahhh', Though I was not sure whether it was from the bungalow or somewhere else, I rushed towards the bungalow.

I ran as fast as possible and reached the rosewood door, which was standing tall and strong, stopping me from entering the bungalow. I tried hard to open the main gate, but all in vain. I tried to find a surrogate entry, but despite taking two rounds of the bungalow, I couldn't find any. I saw that on the first floor of the bungalow there was a balcony, but it was extremely difficult for me to climb it.

In extreme frustration, I kicked the strong rosewood door as hard as I could. I thumped the door with my shoulders too. A sound was all it could produce. My actions were in vain; the gate didn't bother to move in the slightest. After many attempts, I felt tired and took the steps back. I leaned against my Vauxhall Astra, staring at the bungalow and trying to find an entry. I was tapping the bonnet of my Astra when the thought struck me. 'You were there, and I didn't notice.' I said to my car. I had a sudden glint in my eye.

I had planned for a thriller. I resumed my seat behind the wheel in the Astra's and reversed it for a few metres. I then took the safety helmet from the backside of the car, which generally the police patrol team that used the bike wore. Incidentally, one was there in my car. I also put on the seat belt and bent my head as low as possible.

The road was straight, and my car was now positioned just in a straight line to the main rosewood gate of the bungalow. I held the steering tight, and with one leg supporting the break and the other on the accelerator, I warmed up the car a bit. Racing the car, then, to the main door, I banged the car. The car collided with a big crashing sound on the bungalow's door, which gave way. It couldn't bear the high momentum imparted by the accelerated car, and it stood bifurcated. The car witnessed a dent, and the windshield witnessed a blow. The small car couldn't make its way completely inside and got stuck in between. I reversed the car and quickly came out of it. Luckily, the collision did not cause any major injuries to me except for small bruises because of the shattered pieces of the windshield.

The collision had some impact on me as my head was spinning, but the helmet and seat belt prevented me from any major injury. I took a few breaths and then scurried inside the bungalow with my Smith & Wesson 10 pistol in my hand.

Chapter II

GRUESOME MURDERS

The bungalow was dark, and I had to search for my lighter. I found it in the right-hand side pocket of my trousers, and I turned it on. The place glowed a bit, and it was enough for me to search for the switchboard. I switched the main light, and the place radiated. It was the same messy room that I had glimpsed last time: a broken vase, shattered pieces of glass on the carpeted floor, and then I saw the most brutal scene when I walked a little further inside.

The two corpses, whose heads were smashed brutally, and the culprit large boulder was lying nearby. It seemed that the old couple were heartlessly murdered with that large stone by striking their faces time and again. Such a horrific way of giving death. Someone who could be so cruel as to give these oldies such brute treatment—what could he not do with Watson? This thought gave me a chill in my spine.

I rued why I did not throw that girl aside and rush inside the house. Watson was also there with me at that time. We could have prevented the crime. I was not sure whether the girl was trying to warn me of the gruesome crime or if it was a challenge. If it was a challenge, then they didn't know—my name was Richard Carlsen—and I accepted that challenge.

The thought gave me a fresh bout of energy, and I started inspecting the surroundings. I had put on the hand gloves, which were always there with me in my pants' pockets. The two dead bodies seemed to belong to elderly couples. The man would have been aged sixty-five or so, given the wrinkles all around his hands and legs. He was wearing a normal pant and shirt, and his face was mutilated by the hammering it received from that huge stone. The man seemed to wear ordinary dress, and it was nothing flashy or suave, as would have been the case with the gentry residing in these posh areas. The second dead body was of a female who would also be of the same age as that of the dead man. It seemed that the killer didn't want them to be easily recognised, and that's why he had brutally mutilated their faces. It was now difficult to find out who these were. Though a forensic examination could shed some light, I was glad I called the team.

I continued my inspection of that four-story bungalow. The ground floor was well groomed and had all the expensive stuff. The sofa set, large dining table, the central table along with the sofa set, the cupboards, etc. all suited the grandeur of that house. The large living room had a telephone nearby the sofa set, and it seemed that the girl might have called from that phone. The receiver was not kept properly, and it only meant that it was put there in a hurry.

The room was not tidy, and there were some fights, though not necessarily involving the old dead couple.

The deceased body showed no sign of struggle or beating. I could see the blood splashing around the wall where the dead bodies lay. There were many cigars, but they were very similar to what I used to consume. The same Havana cigar butt meant that the murderer was also fond of the same brand of cigars as me. I found it amusing.

I then gave the black-coloured rock a careful look; the murder weapon was soaked in blood. This boulder or rock was brought from a construction site. Such a huge piece of rock would not have been otherwise available in the vicinity. I believe it was a pre-planned murder. The murderer had gotten this huge rock from somewhere far away, and they could easily come into the house, meaning that the murderer and the house owner knew each other well.

I moved further to investigate the bungalow after examining the dead bodies. I murmured, 'A horrible crime.'

I then saw the carpeted stairs and moved through them to the first floor. The area was filled with various paintings, tapestries, photographs enlarged and hung in frames, and exotic stuffed animals. It had all the usual stuff that could be expected in a palatial mansion like that. The interior was well done, and the lighting and false ceiling were squealing the grandeur of the owner of that house.

The floor was well draped by an expensive Persian carpet, though I could see spider nets across the corners. That meant the house was regularly not occupied, and the occupant occasionally used to visit this bungalow.

I moved up the floor through the carpeted stairs and noticed that the paintings, photographs, etc., wherever there was a picture of the owner, were charred. I reached the first floor, and after finding the switchboard, I turned on the lights. I found that the master bedroom was maintained on the first floor, which looked peculiar. Considering that the old couple whose dead bodies were lying on the floor were sexagenarians, why would they have a master bedroom on the first floor? That would cause unnecessary trouble when using the stairs on a regular basis. The ground floor could host the master bedroom easily. Nevertheless, it was possible that the master plan for the bungalow would have been made a decade or so ago when the old couple would not have thought of this inconvenience.

Further, on the first floor in the master bedroom, I saw that the main attached almirah to the wall was ajar, and the clothes and other items were thrown brutally on the ground. When I inspected it closely, I found that there was a locker in the almirah that was intact. I could fathom that there was a try to forcefully open it, but it seemed that the person who made this misadventure was not successful. Because it was highly unlikely that the person who had opened the locker would have closed it back so meticulously. I strolled on the second floor, then the third, and finally the last floor, and found nothing out of the ordinary. While I was inspecting the fourth floor, I heard some noises and took out my Smith & Wesson 10 pistol. I walked with measured steps and slowly descended through the stairs. I was cautious, as it was possible that the culprit or his aide would have returned. I quickly reached the ground floor, and I saw a short man with a fair body and a protruding belly.

'Hello, Mr. Carlsen.' The person said this while looking at my Smith & Wesson 10 pistol. I immediately recognised the voice and the person. 'Melvin, how come you are here?' I questioned.

'You only have called for help.' Melvin responded while coming inside the house completely from the broken door and putting on his hand gloves. I was looking a bit confused, so Melvin continued. 'You have called Louis.'

'Oh. Then where is the team?' I said. I realised that Melvin may be part of the team that Louis would have ordered to reach Bungalow No. 9. Melvin was a police constable who might be on night patrol in that area.

'Ducati 900SS is a delight for the rider.' Melvin pointed out the motorbike parked outside the bungalow's broken gate. He continued, 'Plus, the roads were uninhabited at this hour. The squad can't match my superbike; it will be here any moment.' I nodded and then started looking at the ground floor living room surroundings carefully once again.

'Anything that you have noticed.' Melvin asked.

'Routine. Two corpses, brutally murdered by bludgeon blows by a big rock, a broken vase, charred paintings, Havana cigar's butt, a messy crime scene, and a house that seemed to have been largely unoccupied.' I replied.

'It seems that the murderer did not want to reveal the identity of the victim. Thus, the pain of hitting them brutally with that rock.' Melvin said while pointing at the rock, which now had blood settled on it.

'Yes. What is more peculiar is that the two people did not resist much. Looking at the place where they are lying,' I said, pointing at the two corpses.

Melvin went near the dead bodies, had a closer look, and then said, 'Or maybe first they were sedated with some drugs and then brutally murdered.'

I looked at the corpses closely and found that Melvin's deduction seemed reasonable. The wrinkled dead bodies were lying still when someone was hammering them with that rock. That meant they were sedated.

'There is one more peculiar thing – that weapon,' I added to the mystery.

'Weapon ...' Melvin asked curiously.

I gestured for Melvin to follow me and took him to the carpeted stairs that connected the ground floor with the first floor. After climbing a few stairs, we were at the landing from where the staircase was taking turn. I asked Melvin to look at something that was lying there on that landing.

Melvin picked up the thing and exclaimed, 'An Alfa Combat!'

'Yes. Even I was shocked.'

Melvin started looking at that pistol with a glint in his eyes. Alfa Combat is a Czech-made semi-automatic pistol that was extremely famous with the mafia, and it was smuggled from Czechoslovakia. The mafia was ready to pay a huge sum for possessing one such ruthless killer. Many big businessmen or industrialists too paid a substantial premium over the price to get their hands on this beauty of a weapon.

'We are given this,' I said, pointing at my holster tied to my belt, which had a Smith & Wesson 10 revolver. 'And we are expected to get the better of the criminals holding that,' I said, pointing towards the Alfa Combat that Melvin was holding.

'But Alfa Combat means only one thing...'

'In fact, two things...' I said, correcting Melvin.

Melvin looked confused, and I added further, 'One, as you were rightly thinking, is that the Alfa Combat at this place means the London Mafia is involved in the case, and second...'

Melvin thought of some answer and said, 'The mafia is filthy rich and doesn't care about leaving the Alfa Combat behind.'

I laughed a bit. 'The possessor of this exquisite weapon was in a tearing hurry.'

'How can you say so?' Melvin asked.

'Simple, Melvin. If you have the Alfa Combat and you are taking the pain of bludgeoning those oldies but leaving in such a jiffy that your weapon is left behind...'

'It means that the person had to rush, and the urgency was to leave fast and not something where the person feared any physical harm,' Melvin concluded.

'Yes, the possessor had to rush away. He was not fearing any action but didn't want to be seen. Thus, Alfa Combat was not in his mind when the person was rushing away,' I concluded.

'So, two things are sure: one, the London Mafia is involved in this crime, and second, the person after committing the crime has just left – maybe an hour or so back.'

'Maybe right in front of me.'

'What?'

'Yes. I still rue the fact that I should have forced open the door and stopped the crime when I first met that girl,' I said and went into deep deliberation.

Watson was missing, and I did not know what might have happened to him. If the London mafia was involved, it boded a bad omen. Moreover, someone who could give the old couples such a brutal death could cause inexplicable harm to Watson.

I was still figuring out the three mysteries clouding my mind: the girl calling me to this bungalow – whether she was the same girl I met or they were two different girls. Was this call a genuine shout for help or was it a challenge to the fabled Richard Carlsen? Second, the two security guards were party to the crime, but what was the occasion for them to be disguised as security guards? What were they watching, and why were they stationed as guards? And third, Watson. Where was he missing?

My thoughts were disturbed by a loud thudding sound and the sound of multiple boots tapping the floor. It was the squad that had made its way into the bungalow. The squad consisted of ten members: five policemen and five forensic team members. They were dressed in normal police uniforms, wearing furry black jackets, and each of them had a cocked pistol in their hands, with their hands covered in gloves. The pistols were pointed in all directions, probably because they hadn't spotted me and Melvin yet.

They seemed ready for action, although it wasn't needed. I shouted while leaning forward, 'Relax.' My words changed their gestures. The pistols were holstered, and their stiff postures relaxed.

Louis was leading the squad; he walked towards me and gave a customary salute.

'Thanks, Louis. I am indebted,' I said, pointing towards the squad.

'Mr. Carlsen, your wish was my command,' Louis said poignantly.

I gestured by nodding my head and thanked him.

'Louis, how fast can we identify the dead bodies?' I questioned Louis.

'Aren't they the owners of this house?' Louis countered with a question.

'You see that their heads are brutally bludgeoned, and even the photos which might have their pictures have been burnt,' I replied.

'If you allow me to differ,' Louis said politely.

He could witness the confused look on my face. Even Melvin, who was standing next to me, was confused.

'This entire drama,' Louis continued, 'could be to just make the police think that the victim was someone else.'

'How could you be so sure?' Melvin questioned.

'Because, if the intention was to deceive the police, the murdered would not make it so obvious.' I intervened. I liked Louis because of this. He could think better than the criminal minds. He could read them well. We all had seen the crime scene and thought that the victim's body was mutilated to hide their true identity, but Louis gave it a different perspective.

'I still would like to confirm.' I said looking at Louis.

Louis turned and shouted towards a young-looking person, 'Robert.'

The young person looked at Louis, and Louis gestured for him to come near him and me. The person came and greeted me and Louis.

'This is Robert, team lead for this investigation,' Louis said, gesturing with his hand towards Robert.

Robert nodded his head as if accepting that he was leading the forensic team.

'How soon can we identify these victims?' I asked, pointing towards the two dead bodies.

'Within 24 hours, I will give you the report,' Robert responded.

He was a young person, maybe in his late-twenties, and I was not sure whether such a young person could handle a complex investigation. Louis might have read my mind and intervened, 'Robert is one of the best in the business. Don't go by his innocent looks; he is far deadlier than the devil himself when it comes to forensic evidence gathering.'

Robert blushed.

'Great. Robert, I need all the details, even if they seem innocuous. Also, there is a strange plant grown behind this building in the inner periphery of the bungalow. I want to know what that is,' I authoritatively said.

'Yes, sir,' Robert responded and left us.

'Louis, you have been of exceptional help as always,' I said.

'Thanks, Mr. Carlsen,' Louis replied.

'I am troubled because Watson is missing,' I said. Both Melvin and Louis were looking at me, and they had fathomed that something was troubling me beyond the usual. Therefore, to end their anxiousness, I confessed.

'What?' Louis responded with a shocking voice.

Even Melvin was shocked.

'Yes, Watson and I had come together to investigate the call which gave us a warning about some crime to be committed in this bungalow. When I had gone to call Commissioner Forbes and then you, Louis, it seemed Watson suffered some tragedy,' I said with a sad tone.

'But it is possible that Watson might have been behind the culprit. We just concluded that the crime took place some one hour or so before,' Melvin countered.

'That seems unlikely because the culprit left in front of me in a car. If Watson was following them, he would have been in that Astra,' I said, pointing towards the Astra that had collided with the rosewood door.

'Then it means the perpetrators were not ordinary criminals,' Louis observed.

'Someone who had the audacity to kidnap a policeman, and who possesses Alfa Combat, and who has committed such brutal murders in this posh locality, all indicate at one thing...' Melvin said.

'Involvement of London mafia,' I concluded.

They all were stunned. The London mafia at present was controlled by Sam Ross who used to operate from the shadows. Sam Ross and Henry Walter were the two major kingpins, but after the death of Henry Walter, rather his encounter by London police, Sam Ross became the whole and sole. Later, police realised from various sources that even Sam Ross was working on the directions of someone; some unknown player. In fact, Sam Ross himself had disappeared and now operated from an unknown place. It was a known fact that it was his daughter Lisa Ross who was managing the show on behalf of Sam Ross. Maybe Sam Ross wanted to develop Lisa Ross as his successor. However, Sam Ross himself was not more than fifty and there was no reason to search for a successor – that too a young girl in her early twenties was the most unlikely successor.

I then briefed Louis and Melvin as to what all transpired last night. The mysterious call, mine, and Watson's visit to this bungalow, then the sudden disappearance of Watson, the two hoax guards, and their disappearance in the BMW e-21. The yowl from the bungalow and my rushing there, opening the door forcefully with my Astra.

Louis then proceeded to search the bungalow, and Melvin followed him. I started strolling outside. I was walking along the inner road of the bungalow when I stopped near where the escape vehicle was parked. I spent some time there and realised that the parked BMW e-21 was occupied by the assassin. Maybe Watson was kidnapped by someone sitting in that BMW e-21. The security guards, too, were involved in the crime and fled in that car.

I found my Havana cigar case lying nearby in the grass. I understood that last time I couldn't find my case because the escape vehicle – car was parked there, and now, once the car was gone, I could notice my cigar case. I picked up my Havana cigar, and after cutting the cap from my teeth, I lit it with my lighter. I enjoyed the comforting smoke, and it temporarily relieved me of the pain and grief I was in. Watson was kidnapped, two brutal murders occurred, and the security guard escaped in front of me, all of which were pointing out to the fact that I am losing my sheen. I am Richard Carlsen; I should have done better.

I was standing at the place on the inner road where the BMW e-21 was parked, watching Bungalow No. 9 and enjoying my cigar puffs. The car was very near to the entrance gate where the security guard's cabin was. The boom barrier was erect, which meant that security guard No. 2 did not raise the barrier to allow me to enter but to ensure that the BMW e-21 could easily pass through.

The culprits were sitting in that car all the time while I was running here and there, and the security guard was merely a decoy while the culprits wanted to escape. Was that girl a victim, or was she part of the gang? I needed to find that out. Watson was kidnapped. I then looked towards the other side, the outer road, and thought that if Watson was kidnapped, maybe the guards in the nearby bungalows might have heard something. I was preoccupied by my chain of thoughts that were wandering all across.

I didn't realise when I was outside Bungalow No. 9, wondering what to do next. The hustle and bustle of police action could be witnessed, and many teams were working simultaneously on this double murder. An elderly couple was found dead. This was enough to prompt the dispatch of more teams, and in no time, the isolated bungalow was abuzz with police activity.

I stepped out and started strolling here and there, looking for any trace of Watson. I was still deeply concerned about him. Where had he gone? He was not someone who would leave just like that. I didn't realise that my aimless strolling had taken me to a nearby bungalow, which was around two hundred and fifty metres away from Bungalow No. 9. That bungalow also had a security guard's cabin, and driven by instinct, I stepped inside.

A tall man was seated on a plastic chair with his legs crossed. He had long eyelashes, and his brows were brown, as were his hair. His face had a scar that was not very deep or large. It looked fresh as the wound had recently puckered. He was in a state of sleep, though he didn't seem to be in a deep slumber. His hands showed slight movement, and I politely disturbed him, 'Excuse me.'

The initial attempt was in vain, so I allowed my hands to help me. I moved his body with more force, and his eyes were now open. My black furry jacket hid my uniform, and in the cover of darkness, he couldn't see my police badge either. This made him overlook me and he continued his nap.

'Hey.' My tone grew louder, and his eyes opened again, with gestures showing his irritation.

'What's the matter?' He continued in his irate tone, his confidence reflected in his voice. It was strident, and though it was not to my liking, his manner and demeanour indicated that he was the genuine security guard. He was unlike those two hoaxes I had encountered earlier. One was rustic, and the other was completely out of place to be a security guard.

'I am Senior Police Inspector Richard Carlsen.' I said with authority.

The guard got up and standing in no time. No one could say he was in deep sleep a moment before.

'Yes sir.' He said politely.

Though this guard did not hear the ambulance, and police siren so I doubt whether he would have had any knowledge about Watson's abduction, yet I asked.

'This is how you do your duty.'

'Sorry sir. This is late at night. And we have no work to do here. Most of the bungalows here are vacant. I am sorry sir.' Guard supplicated.

I ignored his excuses and continued, 'I am investigating a case regarding the adjacent bungalow, Bungalow No. 9. My recent tip is that there is an old couple living in the bungalow, and at present, it is uninhabited. The guard escaped after providing me with this information...'

'He fooled you, sir,' the security guard of Bungalow No. 10 cut me off. I wasn't shocked to learn that the information given to me by those two hoax guards was incorrect. He was standing in an attentive position, giving me the respect, a cop so deserved. His etiquette and mannerism suited the security guard of this posh area.

'That house is uninhabited.' The guard politely continued. 'There is no couple living there, but Bungalow No. 9 is owned by an aged man who is unmarried. He occasionally pays a visit here, hardly once or twice a year. This bungalow is completely controlled by his caretaker. The caretaker too comes occasionally and does whatever he is told. There aren't any security guards there.'

I was a bit surprised though I somehow expected the information. Those two security guards were looking completely out of place, and the unkempt way the bungalow was kept meant that the owner visited it occasionally. I found that whatever this guard was saying matched what I could deduce from my observations.

Although I wanted to ask this guard about Watson's disappearance, I knew that someone who didn't bother to notice the sound of an ambulance and police sirens would not have paid any heed to a passing vehicle.

'Who is the owner of this Bungalow No. 9?' I asked spontaneously.

'One Mr. Johnson Allen,' the guard responded.

Johnson Allen. If my memory served me right, he would be the owner of Allen Manufacturing, the salt company which a few years back was on the verge of bankruptcy but somehow in the past two years had made a turnaround.

I needed to inquire further. Was one of the two dead bodies that of Johnson Allen? But then, who was that lady? Why were their faces mutilated, and the photographs burnt? Why did the killer want to hide the identity of the victims? If Johnson Allen was unmarried, then who was that lady, and what was she doing with him at such an hour? Who was that mysterious girl who called me? And last but most important, where had Watson disappeared?

These questions were puzzling me as I thoughtfully strolled back towards Bungalow No. 9.

I strolled back and reached Bungalow No. 9. The police team had placed barricade tape outside the bungalow where the security guard's cabin was. The boom barrier was pulled down. It was almost dawn, and soon, with the sunrise, there would be many visitors who would stop by to look at the police activity at the bungalow. Therefore, the area needed to be cordoned off, and this barricade tape was required to indicate to people that they must not go further, lest they destroy the evidence.

I bent down and crossed the line created by the barricade tape and entered Bungalow No. 9. I had seen that the corpses had been sent for postmortem in the ambulance, and the forensic team was almost done collecting evidence. Robert and his team had done a thorough job.

I was drawn to the plant that was behind the bungalow. It looked like a daffodil, but it was something different. I sat down near that plant and examined the three-foot-tall plant and its flower. Interestingly, I noted that this was the only plant that was well-watered. There were many other plants, but they hadn't been watered for a long time. This meant that the caretaker – as the guard of Bungalow No. 10 had mentioned – only did what he was told, nothing more, nothing less.

'Are you done, Louis?' I said without moving a bit and still staring at the flower of that daffodil-type plant.

'How do you always come to know who is behind you?' Louis questioned.

'Your rose and jasmine perfume is one of a kind. And don't forget...'

'You are Richard Carlsen. The one with an elephantine memory,' Louis said with a laugh.

'True,' I said unashamedly.

'See this,' I added further, gesturing to the flower of that daffodil-type plant.

'What is so special? It seems to be some variety of daffodil,' Louis said callously while towering over the plant.

'Daffodils – especially with white flowers – are rare in this season,' I explained.

'Then it might be some different variety of it,' Louis said. He was still uninterested. He didn't understand why I had such an interest in a plant.

'You haven't noticed that in this huge garden, there were many plants. However, if you see, there are around 10-12 plants of this daffodil.'

'I can see that,' Louis said. He was still uninterested.

'Right. But now notice that only these plants are watered.'

Louis took a deep look at the garden. The crescent moonlight wasn't sufficient to notice such minutiae observations, especially for the uninitiated.

'That means the owner only cared about these plants. The rest were just for show,' I concluded.

Louis was still unsure. 'But how does it help?' Louis questioned.

'My theory is that these plants are extremely important.'

'Because they were watered. What if the owner just liked this type of daffodil?' Louis questioned.

'Well then, the owner would have planted more of them. The owner was extremely cautious that these flowers were few so that they don't catch anyone's attention, like you didn't notice them at all,' I replied.

Louis nodded. He had not even thought about these plants. Now that I had pointed it out, Louis observed them. After all, in this crescent moonlight, it wasn't everyone's cup of tea to observe such minutiae.

'You indeed are a genius. That's why you are Richard Carlsen,' Louis praised.

I blushed, but then the sad abduction of Watson ruined my short-lived pleasure. 'If I were great, I wouldn't have let Watson be kidnapped so easily,' I said with a tinge of sadness in my tone.

'Well, I am afraid you are not thinking in the right direction,' Louis countered.

'What do you mean?' I said with a tinge of surprise.

'I feel that abducting Watson was a risky move for the culprits. Why take Watson with them in that BMW e-21, which, as per you, was the escape vehicle?' Louis questioned.

'Why do you say that, Louis?'

'Because if they had sedated Watson, they could have easily left him in this large bungalow. Best case, they could have locked him inside from the outside. There was no need to carry him in the car.'

'Maybe they wanted to use Watson for some of their purposes.'

'I doubt it. It would have been a far riskier proposition.'

'So, what is your conclusion?' I asked with intent.

'I feel either Watson went after some criminal on his own volition or...'

'Or...' I questioned.

'Or, Watson simply ran away the moment you left. He chickened out.'

'What, Louis? I doubt that,' I said with surprise.

Louis shrugged his shoulders.

I had always appreciated Louis because he had the innate ability to think ahead of criminal minds. He was right; keeping Watson in that BMW e-21 was risky. What if Watson woke up? Nothing stopped the culprits from simply leaving sedated Watson in the large garden or behind many of the parked vehicles, or even better, inside the four-story bungalow.

'I guess you are right, Louis,' I conceded. 'Watson might have been following a culprit or had gone home.'

'If he has gone home,' I added, 'I am not going to leave him.'

'But I still believe in your premonitions. If you feel Watson might be kidnapped, I will circulate Watson's picture in all police stations,' Louis concluded.

I was not sure what to do. If the London mafia was involved and they had kidnapped Watson, they had made a grave mistake. I, Richard Carlsen wasn't an *Hawk eye* accolade recipient year after year for no reason. I was ready to take on the mafia, and if they wanted to make it personal, they would see what mettle Richard Carlsen was made of.

'I want to know the full details about Johnson Allen. It seems this was his bungalow,' I said with authority.

'Sure, I will get it done,' Louis said.

I got busy examining the plant more carefully.

'Don't you want to leave now?' Louis said.

'I will wait for some more time. Maybe Watson will return,' I said with a tinge of sadness.

Louis nodded and stood in his place, watching me play with the leaf of that plant.

Louis and I were examining the small garden behind the bungalow, especially the flower that looked like a daffodil, when our attention was disturbed by a voice. It was Melvin, who was jogging towards us. He said, 'Mr. Carlsen, there is a call for you.'

'Who would call me at this hour and that too here?' I said.

However, before I could say anything further, Louis said, 'At this hour, it's 4.47 AM.'

Louis was known for stating the exact time with no rounding about.

'Mr. Forbes has called,' Melvin replied.

'How did he know the number?' Louis questioned.

'Louis, Notting Hill is a posh area, and you can easily find the number in the yellow pages. Mr. Forbes probably guessed that I am still at this bungalow.'

'Actually, I left a message with Mr. Forbes' office that I am taking the squad at the request of Senior Police Inspector Carlsen.'

'So, you are the culprit,' I mockingly said.

Louis had a scowl, maybe mixed feelings of confusion and guilt. I tapped his shoulder and rushed with Melvin to answer the call.

I reached near the sofa where the two dead bodies had been earlier. Now, the squad had removed them. A constable was holding the phone's receiver, which was near the sofa. I took the receiver and gestured for the constable to leave.

'Hello,' I said.

'Do you have any respect for my orders, Carlsen?' Forbes shouted from the other side of the phone.

'Mr. Forbes, the bungalow...' Before I could finish, Forbes shouted, 'I told you to search it tomorrow, but you asked Louis to go there with the full squad. What if it was a hoax?'

'Sir, there were double murders...'

'I know that. I am being briefed by the team there,' Forbes said.

I wanted to say something, but I decided to keep quiet.

'You need to come urgently to my office,' Forbes shouted.

'Watson is missing...' I wanted to confront, but before I could complete, Forbes said, 'Now means now. I will see you in my office in 30 minutes.' Forbes put the phone down.

What was the hurry? Forbes had asked me to come to his office, not his residence, in 30 minutes. This meant something was serious. Forbes searching for me and taking the trouble to go through the yellow pages and then rushing to his office at 4.50 AM in the morning was not routine.

Louis had also arrived, and he was staring at me incessantly.

'The somnolent man has called me to his office,' I said. 'Right now,' I added with force.

'You can take my Astra,' Louis said and handed me the keys from his pocket.

'Thanks,' I said without any hesitation or false tantrums. I took the keys and rushed out, leaving for the commissioner's office.

Chapter III

THE ATTACK

I got into the Astra and soon zoomed past the residential area. My thoughts were still occupied by the events that unfolded last night. The mysterious call, meeting a strange girl, Watson's disappearance, the two guards helping the culprit and then vanishing from the scene. Everything looked suspicious, and then the brutal murder of an old couple and finding an Alfa Combat at the murder scene.

I was constantly worried about what might have happened to Watson. These thoughts were driving me crazy. In order to divert my attention from these ominous thoughts, I switched on the radio. I knew that Louis loved to hear good songs, and the Astra would soon catch some good music.

To my utmost pleasure, the music band, The Police, was playing Roxanne, and the voice of Sting comforted me the most. I found myself temporarily liberated from the stress. One after the other, great songs were on display, and I was lost in the great world of music. So much so that I didn't realise that the next fifteen minutes zoomed past. I was soon near the commissioner's office.

It was the lane where the commissioner office stood, and I was so engrossed in the music that I couldn't even fathom when a Ford Fiesta came just in front of me, and I experienced a dazzling flash in my eyes. It was a bright light, and my eyes dazzled for a second. When the eyelid opened, I saw a car approaching ferociously towards me. It appeared that the driver of the monstrous car was approaching at an alarming speed due to the driver losing control and was about to bang against my car.

The felonious car was on the wrong side, and to prevent further damage, I had no option but to swerve my car violently towards the right, banging the concrete wall savagely. The driver of the car didn't move but followed the same route. It looked as if he had read my action beforehand. The Ford Fiesta left the scene, following its own path.

The collision gave me a concussion, and I found everything circling around me. It took a couple of minutes before I got normal. I was stuck inside my Astra, which was brutally damaged. The door jammed, and I found it difficult to open. The windshield had shattered and banged against the wall. I couldn't have made any exits from there. I tried to remove the belt from its buckle, but I was unable to. Due to the impact, it got stuck. I sat still and made a few observations. Quickly after, I slipped down from the seat and came out of the belt, slithering like a snake. I tried moving out through the windshield, but I could only succeed in getting my head out.

My left hand was out, and I looked for any sharp object but I failed. I pulled the gun out of the holster and hit the windshield hard with the butt of the gun. The hit wasn't perfect but made sufficient space for me to get out of the damaged car. Though it was around pre-dawn, there were few onlookers on the street. However, despite seeing me struggling to find my way out of the damaged car, none of the onlookers, except one, came forward. The face was a familiar one, but my semi-conscious state prevented any further words of mine.

I saw the familiar face helping me come out of the car, and despite my semi-unconscious state due to the concussion suffered, I could observe that my boss, Mr. Forbes, the commissioner of London police, was in an unexpected place. Forbes had reached the office at the same time, and he saw the accident. He didn't wait and rushed to save me himself.

He pulled my head gently and then pulled from the waist. Another constable had his hands on my head and nape. His hands were cold and rough. With their efforts, I was soon out of the car. He held my arms on his shoulder and asked the constable to help me out. Slowly, with the help of the police staff, I was taken out of the car, and soon I was sitting in the office of Mr. Forbes.

There was a medical attendant who was attending to me, and after some medicines and removal of the shattered glass pieces owing to the two accidents in a span of a few hours, I was feeling alright.

'You must rest, Mr. Carlsen,' the medical attendant with a protruding paunch declared.

I nodded and sipped the water that was brought for me. The medical attendant left, and I was alone with the somnolent man in his cabin.

'Forget about any rest,' Forbes commanded.

'I ain't thinking of any,' I responded.

'What happened?' The commissioner asked while the constable bandaged my wound with a few drops of spirit to cleanse it. Luckily, despite the gruesome scene, I came out largely unscathed. The wounds weren't deep, and the bruises were slight.

I shrugged.

'How come you didn't realise that the Ford Fiesta was rushing towards you furiously, that too in a one-way street?' Forbes inquired.

'I was so engrossed in music that I only realised that monstrous car when it was too late,' I replied innocently.

'Well, while you were getting medical treatment, I found out that the car was not there by happenstance.'

'Then?' I was confused.

'An attempt to take your life.'

'What?' I was shocked.

'Yes, Richard. Commissioner's office lanes are under tight security cover. Had it been an innocent driver, he would not have used this lane without any purpose. Secondly, he would have honked loudly when he saw another car.'

'You are right. I missed that honking part.'

'Yes. Even if we presume that the car's brake failed, it made no attempt to evade the accident.'

'But if we had collided, the Ford Fiesta would have been damaged too,' I questioned.

'Richard, you don't understand. The driver of that killer car was not an ordinary person. He was a trained killer. He would have jumped at the right time and then shot at you.'

'I get it. The person left because he saw you and other constables nearby. Even if he had tried to shoot me then, when I collided with that building, you would have counter fired. So, he better thought to leave,' I summed up.

'Yes, Richard.'

'Therefore, I must be careful.'

'Yes. I have already asked the team to check the details of that car. Unfortunately, I didn't notice its licence plate number.'

'That's okay, I guess the killer will reveal himself soon.'

'Which means, Richard, you have struck the wrong chord. The London mafia is behind you.'

'I have figured that out. I got a call from a girl, and since that call, I guess I am on the radar of the mafia.'

'Seems scary,' Forbes said.

I shrugged. Forbes then further said, 'But they don't know they are messing with Richard Carlsen.'

I chuckled.

'Nevertheless, let's now concentrate on the matter for which I called you,' Forbes said in a serious tone.

'I am curious to learn,' I said.

Forbes pressed the bell, and a constable appeared in the room with a file. The constable left, and Forbes handed over the file to me.

'Go to page seven,' Forbes dictated.

I opened page seven. It seemed to be some kind of report prepared by someone. It had no header or footer and was on plain paper. The title said, 'Drug Mafia Learned the Art of Camouflaging Drugs as Salt.'

The title was interesting, and then I went through the full report. The report indicated how the drug mafia had learned the art of camouflaging drugs as salt. There was a plant that had the property of converting drugs to salt, and the police, even if they caught hold of that drug, could not prove in a court of law that it was contraband.

'Sir, I'm not sure we should rely on the content of this report without any authenticity,' I expressed my doubts, as I was not convinced of the fairy tale process indicated in the report.

'Well, one of my informers has given me this news,' Forbes added.

'I know you are still well connected, but plainly this news is not enough,' I countered.

'Okay,' Forbes nodded his head. He pressed the bell once again, and a constable came into the room.

'Call Alex,' Forbes ordered.

I wondered why, so early in the morning, Forbes had not only called me but also Alex. Alex was the police sub-inspector, and I had worked with him in the past. We gelled well, and it was fun to work together.

Alex entered the room. He was a well-built man, standing around six feet, with a thick moustache that gave him a royal and commanding look.

Alex saluted both Forbes and me and took a seat next to me. Forbes then said to Alex, 'You conducted the raid, and with the help of Dr. Johnathon, you were successful in catching hold of the drugs.'

'Yes, sir,' Alex responded.

'Can you explain it to the great Richard Carlsen?' Forbes said, pointing at the report of drugs camouflaged as salt.

'Sure, Mr. Forbes,' Alex said and then looked at me. I was still confused about what was going on.

'Sir, we received a tip...' Alex began, but Forbes interrupted him with a deliberate cough.

Alex understood the cue and rephrased what he was saying, 'Mr. Forbes received a tip.' Alex looked at Forbes, who now appeared content. Alex continued, 'That a truck was about to enter London city with drugs. Though it will appear as salt, if the right process could be used, we will have proof that these are contraband.'

'Interesting. Mr. Forbes first got this report from an informer and then a tip. And you found out that the Mafia is indeed camouflaging drugs as salt,' I questioned. I remained suspicious.

'Yes.' Alex said to me. He continued, 'I, with the help of Dr. Johnathon, who is an expert on narcotics and contraband, apprehended the truck, and to our surprise, the truck's driver and helper ran away.'

'That doesn't necessarily mean there were drugs. Sometimes these lowly people get scared and run away. Who was the owner of that truck?' I said. I was still firm that drugs can't be camouflaged as salt.

'True, Sir. I did some inquiries with Carlson Marine and Transport Co., the owner of that truck, and they were not aware of any illegal activity. They said it was declared as salt, and their employees ran away because they got scared. They volunteered to help also,' Alex said.

'Then...' I was surprised.

'But then Dr. Johnathon conducted some experiments, and a small quantity was converted back into drugs,' Alex added.

'What?' I said, surprised.

'Yes. Which meant that the salt was drugs. We still have that salt in our police custody,' Alex said.

'And now to cut the long story short,' Forbes intervened, 'I want you, Carlsen, to take it over.'

'I'm not sure what you are saying,' I asked.

'Simple, I've got another tip that another such consignment has arrived today at the London port. I have informed Customs, and they have apprehended the goods. But I want you, Carlsen, to lead this operation.'

'Thanks. I would love to. But, Watson...' I said.

I was cut off. 'It's an order,' Forbes shouted.

'Yes, sir,' I said firmly.

'You both need to immediately go to London Port and get to the bottom of this,' Forbes said. 'This is serious. If the drugs are so well camouflaged, it would be nearly impossible to differentiate between salt and drugs, and we will be in big trouble,' Forbes said with utmost caution.

Alex and I got up, and after a customary salute to Forbes, we left the room. I overheard Forbes asking his secretary to connect with Dr. Johnathon. I understood that Forbes wanted Dr. Johnathon to meet us as well.

Soon, Alex and I were at the parking lot where Alex's Vauxhall Astra was parked. Alex was about to sit in the driver's seat when I said, 'Alex, I'm a better driver than you. Shall I drive?'

Alex looked at me perplexed. 'You and driving don't seem to go well lately,' Alex said politely, looking at the various bandages on my arms.

I giggled and sat in the passenger seat in the front. Alex took the driver's seat, and in no time, we were on our way to the London port.

'Can there be such a process to camouflage drugs with salt?' I questioned.

'I also had my doubts when I first heard, but once you meet Dr. Johnathon, you'll understand it fully,' Alex responded politely.

Before I could say anything, I glanced in the side view mirror. I could see that a Ford Fiesta was following us. I said, 'We're being tailed.'

'What?' Alex looked in the rearview mirror and said, 'This Ford Fiesta just came behind us. I don't think you can conclude that so quickly.'

'Well, did you look at the headlight closely?' I said, still staring at the side view mirror.

'I see there's a small crack in the right headlight,' Alex said.

'The car that was rushing towards me when I was reaching Forbes' office also had its right headlight slightly cracked,' I said.

'What does that prove?' Alex asked, still confused.

'Only this, the chances of an orange Ford Fiesta with a cracked right headlight being on this road from the Commissioner's office to London Port at 6 am—it's too much of a coincidence,' I remarked.

'Hmm,' Alex nodded. He had understood that the killer was behind us.

'Shall I try to catch him?' Alex suggested. We both were cautiously staring at our follower.

'No, let's see what he does,' I remarked.

Alex and I had made a mistake by underestimating our potential killer. He was determined to eliminate me at any cost, and I was not aware of his level of determination or his skill set. Soon, he followed us to the London Port. Alex parked our Astra just outside the Port's entrance.

The Ford Fiesta tailing us stopped a few feet away. It was now confirmed that it was the same car that was following us. I and Alex both got out of the car. However, my right leg got entangled at the foot mat, and I fell down instead of getting out of the car. It was a lucky escape for me. At that moment, a bullet zoomed past me, aimed at my head, and hit the door. A clanging sound occurred, and both Alex and I knew that our killer had fired the bullet aiming at me.

'Richard, please take cover behind the car.' Alex shouted. Alex took out his Beretta M 1951 pistol and fired three shots at our predator. I was behind the car, and the three perfect shots at the Ford Fiesta made our killer run away. Some experts believed that the Smith & Wesson 10 was better than the Beretta M 1951; however, the beauty of any arm is that its prowess depends upon its wielder. Alex was the best in the business, and his shooting prowess was next to none. The killer had no option but to run away from the scene because, had the exchange of fires continued, Alex would have gotten better of him.

'You get inside the port. I will come shortly.' Alex shouted and jumped inside the Astra.

'I shall come with you.' I insisted.

'No, Sir. You go inside the port; that is urgent. I will try to catch hold of this crook.' Alex said. He hurriedly closed both the opened doors and followed the orange Ford Fiesta.

I rushed inside the port, and after showing my identification card, I was allowed easy ingress.

Chapter IV

THE CONSIGNMENT

London Port was among the busiest ports. It handled containers, timber, paper, vehicles, aggregates, crude oil, petroleum products, liquefied natural gas, coal, metals, grains, and other dry and liquid bulk materials. But today, if something was the center of attraction, then it was 'Salt.' The port, bustling with activities even at that morning at 6 am, was gossiping about 'Salt' and how Customs had apprehended an inland waterway boat with drugs, which seemed like salt.

I was in the fifth-floor office of the London Port Authority, from where the entire port and the serene Thames could be seen. The ingress and egress of ships and boats looked picturesque from there.

'Mr. John,' I addressed the short man, dressed formally. He had a short face with beautiful eyes and a Walrus moustache. He lacked a beard, and his brows were as black as ebony, but his hair was brown. A bandage on the right cheek testified that he had recently suffered some injury on the face. His rectangular specs indicated that he was not a man of great taste.

The person was not interested in talking to me and was engrossed in something that he had opened on his Systime computer. The screen had his undivided attention.

He was the port-in-charge of the largest port in the country, if not the world. The port was busy, and even at this morning hour, the hustle and bustle were such that one generally associated with the traffic at the heart of the city at peak time. Many labourers, porters, port staff, marine pilots, etc., were busy with their routines. Everyone was in a steaming hurry.

'Mr. John,' I said with a harsh tone.

Mr. John turned his gaze from the screen towards me and began to recall something. He swivelled in his executive chair and then took off his specs, placing them on the table. The table had nothing but the screen of the Systime computer and some neatly piled files.

'Have we met before?' He asked me, while gently massaging his bandage that occupied a large part of his chin.

'No, I guess not,' I responded.

'How do you know my name then?' John inquired, displaying such a remarkable scowl as if he had asked a significant cross-question.

'Well...' I was about to complete the sentence when a familiar voice took over my words, 'Because Mr. Richard Carlsen saw your name on the black colour board which had the names of all port-in-charges.'

I looked back at Alex.

'The reason I relish your company, Alex,' I said and passed on a small laugh.

Alex laughed too.

John did not understand how two police personnel had arrived in his cabin so unannounced.

'We are here to take over the seized boat from Customs,' Alex said.

John was indifferent. He said, 'What are you doing here?' John gestured with his hand pointing towards his cabin.

'We need some information,' I said.

'I don't have any information that may interest you,' John said.

'Well, let us decide that,' I responded.

John gave a boring stare and started engrossing himself in the computer screen.

'This bandage,' I questioned John, when he again gently massaged the wound covered by the bandage on his chin.

'Nothing exciting,' John responded.

'I would like to know,' I insisted.

'I met with a car accident, a minor one, and this was the result of the same,' he responded with a sigh. He wanted to continue, but Alex interrupted, 'This boat R431...'

'Yes, what about R431,' John asked callously.

'Well, Mr. John, you know that this boat is under police seizure. We have found a lot of illegal stuff there,' I said harshly.

'Yes, I am aware of that, Officer,' John responded. His approach was lackadaisical.

'Then, Mr. John, as port in-charge, can you explain why a boat filled with so much illegal contraband substance was anchored at your port?'

'Officer Richard,' John replied, focusing on my badge and reading my name from there. He continued, 'You are aware that I am in-charge of this port and not of boat R431. Before a boat is docked, I would not know its contents.' John took a page from the pile of files on his table and shoved it towards me.

John continued, 'The declaration stated that boat R-431 has containers of salt from Allen Manufacturers. Now, how do I know whether it was salt boxes or drugs?'

I read the information that the salt boxes were loaded from Grangemouth port of Scotland, and they were coming to London port. They were loaded by Allen Manufacturing's factory at Grangemouth and were headed for the warehouse of the same company in London. They were shipped in the boat that belonged to Carlson Marine and Transport Company, Grangemouth, Scotland.

'And now, officers,' John said while Alex and I were reading the information on the page he had given us. 'You need to excuse me. A London Port in-charge can have everything but what he doesn't possess is....'

'Brains...' I thought to myself, but looking at my facial gestures, Alex understood what I was thinking.

'Time,' John concluded.

I understood that there was nothing that could be extracted from John. I gestured to Alex and said, 'Let's go to the pier then.' We both left in a jiffy from that room.

While we were walking towards the pier, I was engrossed in my own thoughts. If the declaration were to be believed, there were almost a million pounds of illegal drugs camouflaged as salt. Last night, I saw two dead bodies in bungalow no. 9, which, as per the security guard of a nearby bungalow, belonged to Johnson Allen. Now, I am told that the boat was hired by Allen Manufacturing, whose owner, Johnson Allen, presumably was brutally murdered yesterday. Allen Manufacturing used to manufacture salt, and now there was some process by which drugs were camouflaged as salt.

All of these were connecting, and it meant that Johnson Allen was killed because he was involved in a drug racket. That's why Sam Ross gave him the brutal death. Or was it at the order of that unknown boss of the mafia? Was Johnson Allen trying to double-cross the mafia? But how did he manage to get the process of converting drugs into salt?

And most importantly, why did Customs catch hold of an inland vessel? It was not in their jurisdiction. All these confusions were going on in my head, and I did not realise that I had reached the pier. We had walked almost a kilometre from the port authority's office to where R431 was kept captive.

R431 was a narrow boat, which, in my estimation, was around seven feet wide and sixty-five feet long. I could guess that it was a cruiser stern boat. The maximum speed such a boat could achieve was around 14 or 15 knots, and on average, it would be 12/13 knots for the journey. That meant if the boat was coming from Grangemouth and reached London port, it might have taken almost 35 hours or so if they had not stopped anywhere.

That meant the boat had started from Grangemouth before the brutal murder of Johnson Allen – presuming one of the deceased last night was Allen. I was doing all these mental calculations when I saw Alex had already embarked upon the boat and was signalling me to come up.

I climbed up the three small stairs and was on the deck of the boat. I saw one place was marked, and there were two customs officials standing. I presumed they were waiting for the local police for the handing-over. I and Alex went to them, and they saluted me as the official protocols indicated that I was higher in the hierarchy.

'How come Customs seized an inland boat coming from Scotland to London?' I inquired.

'Sir, we received an order from the Commissioner of London Police,' the Customs' official responded politely. He was in his mid-twenties and seemed to have just joined the force. The other was even junior to him.

'Mr. Forbes ordered you,' I asked, surprised.

'He had received a tip. Someone had to act; the local police were taking time, and thus we acted,' the Customs official said hurriedly.

I was surprised, but I nodded and went on to inspect the boat. Alex got engaged with them to complete the handing-over formalities.

I noticed that there were huge consignments covered in a thick blue plastic cover. One of the consignments was forced open, meaning that the Customs officials might have opened it to check. There were small sachets, and on closer examination, they seemed like salt.

I opened one sachet and took the white material in my palm. I tasted it, and it was clear that it was not salt. Though the material was giving me a kick, it would be difficult to prove in a court of law that it was any contraband.

This meant that the report received by Forbes was not wrong. Someone had done deep research in London's drug mafia, and that mole had revealed the biggest secrets of this mafia.

I strolled further and looked at the huge stock of consignments. I also noticed that there was an empty gun flare. It looked strange to be on that boat. There was a marking as if some dead body had been kept there.

I took my cigar and lit it while taking a few strides here and there. The Customs officials had gone, and Alex came near me. He accidentally inhaled my cigar's smoke and coughed.

I moved in a different direction not to cause harm to him.

'What happened to our guest, whom you followed?' I inquired.

'He ran away in some alley. I couldn't find him, so I thought instead of wasting time, I must return,' Alex responded.

'Hmm. Did you see the salt?' I questioned.

'Not yet. But I presume you have seen,' Alex replied.

'Yes. And indeed, whatever was written in that report by that informer of Forbes was right. I presume it is the same informer who informed about this boat.'

'Yes, Richard. I checked with the Customs officials. Last night, Forbes received a call.'

'What time?' I interjected and asked.

'Around 3.30 PM or so,' Alex replied.

'Oh,' I said and then went into thought. Was it possible that it was the same girl who called me, who was Forbes's informer?

'Forbes informed the Customs officials, and then he called you and me to take over the case,' Alex continued.

As we discussed, a few thud sounds grew louder, and we approached the source of the noise. An old man was spotted climbing the ladder. Alex helped him, and he came up on the boat deck.

'Hi, Dr. Johnathon – Chief Scientist of Narcotics Control Dept.,' he introduced himself, with a small bow and raising his hand for a handshake. I shook his hand and responded, 'Richard Carlsen, Senior Police Inspector – London Police. He is Alex, Sub-Inspector – London Police.' I pointed towards Alex.

Dr. Johnathon coughed a bit. He stood beside me, and I focused on him, an aged person. His bald head had a few white hairs. He moved towards the open box of the consignment and took the sachet just opened by me in his hand. He examined it deeply and then smelled the packet.

He handed over the small sachet to Alex to hold, and he took out a test tube from the inner pocket. He allowed a few grams of the contents of the sachet into the test tube. From the inner pocket on the other side of his blazer, he took a dropper and allowed a few drops to fall freely into the test tube. The hazy white-coloured sample had now turned into pure white.

He then emptied the content into my palm and said, 'Senior Police Inspector Carlsen, can you tell me what this substance is?'

I was a bit perplexed. Nevertheless, I smelled it. The smell was odourless, and the substance was pure white. It looked like powdered sugar, but I, from my experience, can tell that it was – 'Pure cocaine,' I answered.

'Right. Can you say that with certainty earlier?' Dr. Johnathon questioned.

'No. But I can now.'

'Yes. Now even if you test it in some lab, it will be proven that it is pure cocaine, and such a huge quantity of cocaine smuggling is illegal, punishable with the severest punishment,' Dr. Johnathon concluded. He moved around and looked at the boat all around. He then said, 'If this boat was not apprehended, a huge amount of cocaine would have been circulating on the streets of London.'

'That too without any risk,' I added.

'Yes.'

'Can you tell me what kind of liquid you added that converted the salt back into cocaine?' I inquired.

'First up, it was not salt. It was pure cocaine, which, with the help of the latex of the Lakshmi plant, was disguised as powdered sugar,' Dr. Johnathon added.

'Lakshmi plant.' Both Alex and I said in unison.

'Yes. And it was not salt but more akin to powdered sugar.'

'I guess since Allen Manufacturing is registered to manufacture salt, they declared it as salt,' I intervened.

'Probably,' Dr. Johnathon said. He was not much into investigative work; his specialty was hardcore narcotics study.

'But what is this Lakshmi plant?' I questioned.

'Well, some two years ago, Prof. Lakshmi Trust of Edinburgh University – Dept of Botany did an interesting discovery, and her paper was much appreciated. She discovered that there is this hybridized mutant plant of the Narcissus genus, and its latex can be used as the perfect anaesthetic.'

'We haven't heard about it,' I interjected.

'Yes,' Dr. Johnathon said. 'Maybe because Lakshmi Trust was abducted by the Henry Walter gang.'

'Oh.' Both Alex and I said in unison.

'Yes. And then it seemed that Walter forced Lakshmi to use that plant to camouflage cocaine as powdered sugar,' Dr. Johnathon said.

'Walter was killed in an encounter,' I said.

'Yes,' Dr. Johnathon said.

'And that too by Watson,' Alex added.

'But since then, no one has heard about Prof. Lakshmi,' Dr. Johnathon said.

'If I have to summarise,' I added, 'Prof. Lakshmi discovered a plant that will help camouflage cocaine as powdered sugar or salt, and then she was abducted by Walter. Walter was killed by Watson in an encounter, and then maybe Sam Ross abducted Prof. Lakshmi.'

'Yes, and then Prof. Lakshmi was forced by Sam Ross to disguise the salt prepared by Allen Manufacturing,' Alex added.

'Precisely,' I said and continued. 'For the past two years, Johnson Allen was making money because he was helping Sam Ross. Prof. Lakshmi was in their confines.'

'Well, officers, these are your domains. I can't add much to it,' Dr. Johnathon said.

'How does this plant look like?' I asked.

'A single flower plant on a long green stalk, with green leaves growing from the base of the stem. The flowers have a strange iridescent petal surrounding a trumpet, which has the same iridescence. Lakshmi plants grow between 40 to 50 centimetres tall,' Dr. Johnathon described.

'It looks more like a Daffodil then. White petals surrounding a trumpet and 50 centimetres tall,' I put across my point of view.

'Yes, Mr. Carlsen. In fact, a Daffodil too belongs to the Narcissus genus; it also has properties of trance,' Dr. Johnathon added.

Now the picture was clear. The plant that I saw last night at Bungalow no. 9 was the Lakshmi plant. It appeared to have white petal Daffodil, but in fact, it had iridescent-coloured petals.

'If I may ask for the liquid in that bottle, which you used to convert the salt back to the drug,' I said with childlike anxiousness.

'Mr. Carlsen, that is nothing but the crushed flower of the Lakshmi plant, which undoes the impact of its latex,' Dr. Johnathon said.

'The process then is to use the latex of the Lakshmi plant, and then the cocaine would be disguised as salt, and to undo it, use the flower juice of the same plant,' Alex intervened.

'Well, in theory, yes, but it requires a huge processing. Yes, for a small quantity, you can convert it back by mixing it with flower juice, but to camouflage large quantities, you need a large factory,' Dr. Johnathon said.

'More so there are other parameters, right pressure, right temperature, maybe some catalyst chemicals, etc.,' I added.

'Yes, Mr. Carlsen,' Dr. Johnathon said.

The picture was clear now in my mind. Johnson Allen and Sam Ross were hand in gloves. Lakshmi Trust was abducted, and she was forced to help disguise cocaine as salt. Allen manufacturing was sending that salt-looking cocaine, and the police were not in a position to catch hold because no one could prove it was cocaine. Thus, in the past two years, all was going great.

But then that mysterious informer of Forbes informed Forbes a few days back about this salt-like drug and then also gave information about a truck. Alex caught hold, and then Sam Ross and the London mafia sent the goods through a boat. But now the boat also was apprehended.

Was that mysterious girl I met in Bungalow no. 9 was the informant? Who was that girl who opened the door? I clearly remember each and every detail of her.

'I must make a move,' Dr. Johnathon said. His voice disturbed my thought process.

'Yes, sure Dr. Johnathon,' I said. 'You were of great help. Can I take that bottle from you?' I insisted.

Dr. Johnathon gave me the small bottle which had a little liquid left. He then waved his hands and left the boat carefully. The Customs officials standing down at the dock helped the old sexagenarian Dr. Johnathon, and he left the scene.

'Alex, what information have you gathered about the crew of the boat?' I asked.

'Well, it seems there were three of them on the boat. As soon as Customs announced around 4 am that they were under seizure, one of them fired a flare and jumped into the Thames.'

'What a daredevil. But why did he fire the gunshot for the flare? Generally, it is done to give some signals.' I said.

'Difficult to tell right now. But he jumped and swam, and somehow could not be caught.'

'Oh. So, one of the three accused left. What about the other two?'

'Another one tried to jump, but it seems he didn't know how to swim and, in his anxiety, drowned. He died a painful death.'

'That's strange. A boat crew did not know how to swim,' I said with a suspicious tone.

'Maybe he was a last-minute addition. The third also chickened out looking at the painful death of his colleague and better thought to surrender to Customs.'

'Oh. So, he is in Customs' custody.'

'Now handed over to us.'

'Then let's find out what he knows. You bring him here,' I ordered.

'Sure,' Alex said and left. He gestured to the Customs officials and, through sign language, told them that the accused who was caught was summoned by me at the boat deck. They gestured, saying they would bring him soon.

I was just wondering about the new discoveries and how everything was connected. It was a coincidence that Forbes gave me this new case, but it was so well connected with Bungalow no. 9. It seemed that Johnson Allen and Sam Ross developed some kind of friction leading to the murder. But then who was that lady? Was she Lakshmi Trust? But why would Sam Ross kill both Johnson Allen and Lakshmi Trust? Furthermore, where was Watson? It was highly unlikely that Watson was abducted for more than eight hours now, and there was no news of him. I was wondering whether Watson was alive, or the brutal mafia had ...

Then I mentally decided not to let such negative thoughts cloud my mind. The biggest enemy of any detective was fear. Fear clouds your judgement. Detectives had to remain objective and verify each fact and not conclude anything or rule out any possible scenario.

My thoughts were disturbed by the small thuds. The person who was arrested in handcuffs was brought to the boat, and the constable of Customs was holding the rope. Alex said, 'He was arrested. He was the third person. One fled, one dead, he remained.'

I looked at the person. He was extremely skinny, hardly covered in a thin pant and shirt, despite October's cruelly cold temperatures, and he had made a long boat journey over the North Sea and the River Thames.

'What is your name?' I shouted.

'Da.. mm.. vid,' he said almost bleating.

'David – is it?' I barked.

He nodded. He was trembling with fear or maybe cold. I was not sure. He had spent almost one and a half days at sea in that narrow boat with such thinly clad clothes.

'You work with which gang? Who gave you these drugs?' I shouted.

He was silent. He didn't answer.

'Speak up,' I shouted as furiously as I could.

He was unmoved. He was not willing to say anything.

'You speak, else...' Alex said and handed him a tight slap.

I was shocked. But I kept mum. David was injured by that slap, but he still was not willing to say anything.

'You either speak or else we have to be extremely brutal,' I said.

'I don't know anything,' David finally said.

'So, you could speak. I thought for a moment you were dumb,' I mockingly said.

He did not respond. He was standing, keeping his gaze down to earth.

'Why did you three try to escape? If you had done no wrong,' I inquired.

'Sir, we got scared,' David replied.

'But why?'

'Sir, we thought that Customs would arrest us. We didn't have any permit? Nobody told us that Customs would be there.'

'For this small thing, a fellow of yours would jump in the Thames and willingly take such a painful death,' I shouted.

'You liar,' Alex slapped him again.

David got a cut on his lips, and it was bleeding, but he did not say anything.

'Ok. Alex, he is of no use. You throw him in the Thames. I guess there is no record of his arrest,' I said, looking at Alex in a high tone.

David was overhearing me but was not reacting.

'We have made no record yet,' Alex responded.

'Good. Throw him in the water, if need be, shoot two or three bullets. Rather ask the Customs fellow to shoot bullets. Show that he tried to escape and got killed,' I concluded and started descending from the boat.

Alex took out his Beretta M 1951 pistol and gestured to the police constable. The constable dragged David with the help of the rope, and soon David was on the verge of the deck. The constable then got hold of his legs and was about to lift.

'What are you doing?' David shouted.

'Just easing your misery,' Alex responded.

'No, please,' David pleaded.

'Well, you are of no help. And keeping you alive doesn't serve our purpose. Too much paperwork,' Alex said.

The constable was trying hard to throw David into the Thames. Alex also reached to help. Alex was a stout person, and in no time, he had taken skinny David in his lap. Alex was about to throw David into the Thames.

'Wait, please wait...' David shouted. He was perspiring like anything. His blood pressure might have shot up.

Alex waited for a minute.

David was panting. I knew how much it would take for David to finally break, and thus I was already climbing the stairs to reach the deck of the boat.

I saw Alex and the Customs constable standing near David, and he was sweating and panting.

'I don't have time,' I barked.

'Sir, I don't know much. Only that we were told to carry this salt consignment from Grangemouth to London Port,' David said while still panting.

'Then why did you run away,' I inquired.

'Sir, I am not much aware, but our captain who was in control of everything, he jumped in the river and ran away. He also fired the flare-gun, maybe to indicate that he was in danger.'

'You weren't aware of anything,' I questioned.

'No, sir. I and that other colleague, we both didn't know anything. The captain ran, so my partner also thought to run away as he was scared. I also wanted to run away but I don't know how to swim and thus got arrested,' David said. He was now breathing almost normally.

Alex wanted to slap him again, but I gestured not to. Alex stopped.

I left the boat and gestured Alex to follow me. Alex followed. David was in custody of that constable, and both of them were at the boat deck.

I descended down along with Alex.

'He doesn't know much. He is stating the truth,' I said.

'Ok, sir. Then what is the plan,' Alex asked.

'Nothing. We can't do much here. Take the boat, the goods, and this David in custody. Ask someone from the team to do the paperwork.'

'But Allen Manufacturing's lawyer will easily come and get these goods and David released. We can't prove these are contraband,' Alex inquired.

'I know. We will find out some solution. But for now, let's proceed on the assumption that the entire consignment is cocaine or other contraband,' I firmly said.

'Ok, sir,' Alex responded.

'I'll leave for home, and you take care of things here,' I said.

'No, sir. I will drop you. The killer is at large,' Alex said.

'But here the formalities...'

Before I could complete the sentence, Alex said, 'The custom officials are my friends. They can manage for some time. I will drop you home, come back, and complete formalities.'

'Ok.'

Alex went up to the boat, said something to the constable there, and then he rushed to the Customs' office at the London port, and in some time, he came back. We both then reached the parked Astra outside the port. Our killer guest was not to be seen, nor his orange Ford Fiesta. Alex dropped me home, and he did not leave until Emily, my wife, opened the door and took me in.

Chapter V

THE MYSTERIOUS GIRL

Emily, my wife, comforted me. She knew that I had an extremely long day. Emily was around my age in her mid-thirties. She stood at five feet seven inches, had sharp features, a well-built figure, natural blonde hair, and, contrary to popular perception, a beautiful blonde with an extremely sharp mind. She was a crime reporter and had conducted interviews with all the big-shot mafias, whether it was Henry Walter, Sam Ross, or Forbes – the Commissioner of Police used to provide her with lots of soundbites.

She met me, and I admired her beauty with brains attitude. What she saw in me was doubtful, perhaps my legend – the *Hawk-eyed* super detective – Richard Carlsen the great. We had been happily married for the past three years. We didn't have any children yet, but that was never a concern for either of us. I believed that Emily understood me far better than any of my criminal nemesis or police friends.

I took Emily in my arms, but before I could say something, Emily pointed towards a lady sitting on the sofa set in our living room. It was 8:30 AM, and it was early for a guest. I could see her from behind, and I was curious about this early morning visitor.

'Ms. Taylor has come to meet you, Richard,' Emily said, holding my hand and leading me to the sofa where Ms. Taylor was sitting.

'Hi, Ms. Taylor,' I greeted her. Ms. Taylor was around ten years older than Emily, just as Watson was ten years my senior. Ms. Taylor appeared petrified, and I was unsure of what to say.

'Tell me the truth, Richard,' Ms. Taylor said, her eyes teary and her tone weepy.

'I beg your pardon,' I responded.

'Please, Richard. Ms. Taylor is extremely disturbed. Don't play games,' Emily said with irritation.

I wasn't sure whether Ms. Taylor knew about Watson's abduction or suspected it. Or perhaps there was some other news that had her so upset. I chose to ignore Emily's comment and asked Ms. Taylor again, 'Ms. Taylor, you may need to tell me the complete story so that I can help.'

Ms. Taylor burst into tears, and Emily was taken aback by my attitude. She handed Ms. Taylor a glass of water. I remained in a dilemma. I didn't want to break the news to her that her husband was missing, as it would cause more trauma. Unless, of course, she already knew. The way she was behaving seemed to suggest that she did, but I didn't want to take chances.

'Louis called me,' Ms. Taylor said after controlling her emotions. Emily was sitting next to her, rubbing her back gently.

I understood what was coming next.

'He asked for Watson's pictures so that he can circulate them to various police stations. He told me

Watson has been missing since last mid-night.' Ms. Taylor said everything in a clear tone. She was looking at me as if I were the culprit.

'Richard, please don't hide facts,' Emily said in a stern voice.

I didn't like this aspect of Emily; she unnecessarily became too bossy at times.

'Ms. Taylor, no one knows for sure that Watson was missing. He might have gone after the criminals.'

'Richard, can you explain from the beginning?' Emily intervened.

I knew that unless I satisfied Emily's queries, she would not let me speak to Ms. Taylor.

I said, 'Last night, around midnight, I received a call from a girl who told me that a gruesome crime was going to happen at Bungalow No. 9, Notting Hill Residential Area.'

Ms. Taylor was not interested in these details, but I could sense that Emily had donned the hat of the crime reporter she was. I ignored the sentiments of both these ladies and continued, 'I thought it was a hoax, but Watson insisted that I must address the call. He forced me to visit the place where the crime was about to be committed.'

'You didn't want to investigate something – the famous Richard Carlsen, but Watson insisted. Interesting,' Emily intervened again.

Ms. Taylor was feeling suffocated as she could not withstand the drama going on between us, husband and wife. Nevertheless, I continued.

'I reached there, a girl opened the door, but then she shut the door bluntly, asking me to get the search warrant. I went to call Forbes from a nearby telephone booth, leaving Watson behind. When I returned, neither Watson was there nor the guard who had met me. I met a new guard.'

'So, it was a set-up. You shouldn't have gone to arrange a search warrant. You should have barged in when the girl opened the door,' Emily again intervened.

'But, Emily, I wasn't sure whether any crime had been committed. Moreover, barging in without backup would have been risky for both me and Watson,' I responded.

Ms. Taylor was looking at both of us, flabbergasted. I could tell that she was now getting extremely angry. I said, 'Emily, I will explain the details to you later.'

I then looked at Ms. Taylor and said with softer tone, 'Ms. Taylor, when Watson connects with me, I will let you know.'

I thought I had given her some comfort, but she went into absolute shock. She had not said anything earlier, but now she wasn't even listening. She lay on the sofa, and Emily gestured for me to go inside the room.

Without uttering a word, I went inside the room. I heard Emily saying to Ms. Taylor, 'Don't worry, Watson will be safe.'

I shut the door. I was extremely tired. Without changing my police uniform, I lay on the bed and fell asleep in no time.

I didn't realise it, but I had been sleeping for almost an hour when I heard banging at the door. I opened it, and it was Emily. 'The Police Commissioner Forbes is on line. He wants to speak to you urgently,' Emily said hurriedly.

'Oh, okay.' I got up and rushed to the living room. Ms. Taylor was not there, but Emily pointed through her fingers, indicating that Ms. Taylor was resting in another room. I nodded and picked up the receiver.

'Get ready. There is another boat coming to London port with the same consignment,' Forbes said with intent.

'What?' I was shocked. Two consignments on the same day within a matter of hours.

'I will reach London port immediately,' I said.

'No,' Forbes said. 'I am aware of the threat to your life. Alex is on his way.'

Before I could say anything, Forbes disconnected the call.

Emily was behind me. She said, 'another consignment at London Port.'

I was shocked. How did she know?

'Simple, I overheard a few words and could guess the rest,' Emily said innocently.

She was a sharp girl. Emily poked, 'Then what happened last night? Did you find anything at the Bungalow.'

I always hated Emily prodding too much. But I loved her, and I knew that she had sacrificed her career, but she couldn't take her investigative journalist DNA away. I thus always explained everything to her. In fact, many of my colleagues said that someday, if Emily goes to the police station instead of me, she could handle my work.

'Nothing much. But I found an Alfa Combat.'

'Alfa combat. That means your adversary is extremely dangerous,' Emily said.

'Yes. Also, I got a tip from Forbes that some salt consignment was coming. So, I went to London Port.'

'Salt consignment is no crime, Richard,' Emily said shockingly.

'In fact, the London Port's in-charge also was behaving strangely, precisely due to this reason. He believed that the police were apprehending someone who got salt.'

'Well, I will not blame him,' Emily said.

'But, Emily, the drug mafia had gotten hold of a process whereby they could convert cocaine into salt or a powdered sugar-type substance.'

'What? I don't believe that, Richard,' Emily said.

'Yes, Emily. And that's why it was difficult to prove that it was cocaine.'

'But then the kick; will it be similar to cocaine?' Emily questioned.

'Yes. The disguised cocaine, which looked like salt, would be sold at an extremely high price, and it will create the same addiction as cocaine. Whenever we catch hold of these substances, the defence lawyer would take a technical plea that these substances are not cocaine or any other contraband, and the court would acquit the culprits in the absence of concrete evidence.'

'That is a smart plan, Richard,' Emily exclaimed.

Before we, husband and wife, could discuss the matter further, there was a ring at the door.

It was Alex. He was spot on time. Emily greeted him and brought him straight to the living room. Alex had a file, and he sat down. Alex said, 'Mr. Forbes wants you and me to be at London Port.'

'Let me just freshen up, take a quick bath, change clothes, and then we will leave,' I said politely.

'Ok. I will wait,' Alex said.

Emily said, 'I will prepare coffee for you two and something to eat. You both should eat a little and then leave.'

Alex wanted to say something but then decided against it. Emily was a good cook too. I rushed to take a bath, and Emily got busy in the kitchen. Alex was sitting in the living room on the sofa and reading the file he had brought. It was primarily the map of London Port and nearby areas.

Soon, I came out, and Emily had also prepared coffee and sandwiches. The three of us sat at the sofa set when I told Alex, 'Yes, tell me what you've got.'

Alex wondered that Emily was sitting there. He hesitated. I intervened, 'Don't worry, Alex. Emily knows everything. In fact, she only answered the call from Mr. Forbes. We can discuss in front of her.'

Alex nodded. Emily had a glint in her eyes. She wanted to be part of such conversations.

'Mr. Forbes received another tip,' Alex continued.

'What? Forbes is still so connected with his network that he receives tips directly,' Emily intervened.

'Yes. Forbes was a celebrated cop, and yet he has a strong network,' I answered.

'And thus, I got you the full map of London Port and also the surrounding areas,' Alex said.

Alex then opened the file and the map. He continued, pointing at the map, 'From Grangemouth, Scotland, where Allen Manufacturing Co. has its large factory, the salt is produced, which is then given the shape of a drug, and it is shipped through Carlson Marine & Transport Co.'

'Interesting, Richard. There is a Carlson Marine and Transport Co. too. Your surname is popular,' Emily mockingly said.

Alex and I both ignored her, and I looked at Alex to continue.

'Grangemouth port is around four hundred and sixty miles, and from various cruiser stern narrowboats, this salt or cocaine is shipped to London Port. From there, it is sent to the warehouse of Allen Manufacturing Co. in London and then to various drug dealers.'

'They could use road transport. That would be faster,' Emily chimed in.

'Yes, Emily. But they were primarily using road transport for the past couple of years, but then Forbes received this tip and since then...'

'London police made it difficult for these mafia lords,' Emily intervened and concluded.

We both nodded.

'So, what is the tearing hurry that brought you here,' I asked Alex.

'Forbes has received another tip.'

'Understood. Another boat is coming. But that is surprising.'

'Yes, Richard. The first boat was apprehended around 4 am, and now at 10 am, another boat,' Alex said.

'Well, dear cops, I feel this is usual,' Emily said.

Both Alex and I were surprised.

'The mafia would generally send the goods in two or three parts,' Emily continued, while Alex and I were watching her with intent. 'This is to ensure that even if one of their own captains turns rogue, they don't lose out in full. Moreover, in such eventualities when one such boat is apprehended, the other has time to run away.'

'I understand now the purpose of that flare,' I said.

'Yes, Richard. Gun flares generally are the signal to indicate that there is danger,' Emily said.

Both Alex and I were looking at Emily in awe. Though she was too nosy, her insights about the drug mafia or criminal minds in general were extremely helpful. She had been a celebrated crime reporter, and some three or four years back, she would be the best in the business. Therefore, I also never mind engaging with her. She at times becomes too bossy and nosy, but then everything had pros and cons.

'We must leave asap,' I said.

'Yes. According to Forbes, the second boat must have reached by now. The tip suggested the landing time as 11 am on 6th October,' Alex said.

'And it is almost 11. Let's leave,' I said.

I rushed and got ready. I adorned the new set of my uniform, checked my Smith & Wesson 10 pistol, and also kept some extra bullets. Alex was already ready. I gestured to Emily about Ms. Taylor, and Emily indicated through gestures that she was sleeping in the next room. I kissed Emily and left with Alex.

We reached London Port, and after waiting for an hour, there was no suspicious movement—no boat, nothing. We inquired, and we were told that another boat from Carlson Marine and Transport Co. was scheduled to arrive around 11 AM at London Port, but it hadn't reported yet.

It was almost 12:30 PM when I told Alex, 'Arrange for a cigarette boat. We are going to Grangemouth.'

'What?' Alex questioned.

'Yes. Please do it fast,' I said.

'Ok.' Alex left to arrange for a cigarette boat.

A cigarette boat runs much faster in the sea than a narrow boat. The distance of four hundred and sixty miles from Grangemouth to London, which a narrow boat may take thirty-six hours to cover, could be done in just eight to nine hours by the cigarette boat.

Alex was efficient and arranged for the cigarette boat quickly. In no time, he and I were in the boat, and I was driving it. I had driven such boats many times, so it was nothing new for me. Alex was still perplexed.

'Alex, focus on timing, and you will understand my action,' I said to give him some clue.

Alex went into deep deliberation and then said, 'You mean that around 4 am, the first boat arrived from Grangemouth. It means it might have started around thirty-six hours, which is around 4 PM on October 4.'

'You are approaching it right,' I added. I was driving like a pro, and Alex was mesmerised looking at my driving skills. I could drive any vehicle, whether on the road or at sea. Alex was not aware of this skill of mine. He went back to his calculations.

'As per Emily, the mafia might have sent the second shipment after a few hours, say at 10 pm, and it would reach here around 10 am,' Alex said.

'Yes, Alex. And around 4 am, Customs, on the request of Forbes, caught hold of the first boat. The person left and fired a flare shot—a distress signal.'

'But the other boat might be 80 to 100 miles away by that time. It would be difficult for them to watch it.'

'Alex, how are you so sure that there was not a third boat? There could easily be a third cigarette boat, like ours, who was watching these shipments,' I questioned.

'You are right, Richard. Probably after the truck seizure, the mafia might have learned their lessons,' Alex added.

'Yes, Alex. That's why the person jumped into the Thames, and he knew that he would be saved. Otherwise, no sane person would jump in the middle of the river knowing that it was impossible to keep swimming for hours.'

'He knew some help would come.'

'Yes, Alex.'

Alex now understood why Richard was given the matter. Forbes knew that if anyone can solve this puzzle, it would be Richard. His experience, approach, and thought process were beyond anyone. He could see and fathom things that none of the officers could do.

'Where are we heading to,' Alex questioned.

'We are going to Harwich Port,' I answered.

Alex's facial expression changed.

'Don't flinch, dear. If we are lucky, we would encounter that boat with salt cum drugs in between,' I said.

I started the journey, and soon I diverted to Harwich Port. Alex questioned, 'Why Harwich?'

'If my estimation is not wrong, those people might have left this boat at Harwich Port on some pretext and had run away.'

Alex was looking confused.

'See, Alex, they were running from the police and Customs. They were in a narrowboat that could not match the speed of a cigarette boat, which generally these officials have. So, the best course was to leave the boat as soon as possible and run away. They might have left the boat either in the mid-sea or at best near Harwich Port, which is around eighty-five miles or so from London Port.'

'Richard, you calculate fast. This means when the first boat was apprehended around four in the morning, the other boat would be around Harwich Port,' Alex ejaculated. He was impressed by my skills, and the same was clearly visible on his face.

'Thanks,' I said.

Alex now understood why I was studying that map so deeply when he brought it to my house. I was finding the escape route that the second boat crew would use.

Soon, we were near Harwich Port, and I could see the boat stranded. Alex got thoroughly impressed. That's why I was getting the *Hawk-eye* accolade year after year. We, with the help of local port authorities, parked the boat. The crew members of the boat might have run away. Presumably in that cigarette boat, which might be there to help these two boats.

David was the only crew member that we have got with us. Others had fled away, and one unfortunately died. I was sure that these lowly crew members would have gone and by now told their bosses that their boats had been seized by the London police.

The Forbes informant, in a matter of hours, had caused a huge loss to Sam Ross. The cocaine, I estimated, in this second boat would also be worth around a million pounds.

Was it that girl who was behind it? But how did she manage to intimate Forbes about these two boats? According to Forbes, he received the call around three in the morning. She was in their custody last night at that time. It was all a huge suspense.

Alex was busy with the formalities. We had the declaration for this boat, which was on similar lines. Allen Manufacturing Co. had shipped salt through the boat registered with Carlson Marine and Transport Co., Grangemouth. The goods were shipped from the Grangemouth factory of Allen Manufacturing Co. to the London warehouse of the same company.

I went to a local phone booth and dialled Forbes. This time Forbes answered on time. It was around 4.30 PM, so it was expected.

'This is Richard,' I said.

'Yes, Richard. What is the news?' Forbes inquired.

'We have apprehended the second boat too. It was stranded near Harwich port.'

'Harwich port?' Forbes asked. He had a tinge of confusion in his voice.

'The first boat was caught by Customs around four AM in the morning. The second boat, which was following it, was around Harwich at that time. According to my theory, there was a third boat – a cigarette boat – which saw the flare signal and went back to intimate the second boat crew to run.'

'So, they all ran away. But you got the boat.'

'Yes, sir. Not only the boat but almost a million pounds worth of cocaine.'

'What? A million pounds.' Forbes got the shock of his life.

'Yes. So, in a matter of hours, your informer had ensured that the drug mafia suffered more than two million.'

'And don't forget the truck,' Forbes said with pride.

'Yes, sir. If I add the truck also, that means the drug mafia is down by more than two and a half million pounds.'

'That will break their backbone. It was a huge loss.'

'The leakage of this news to your informer and the apprehension of that truck might have caused the death of Johnson Allen last night in Bungalow no. 9,' I added.

'What? Is there any connection between your last night's investigation and this?' Forbes questioned.

'Yes, sir. As your informer has told you, the drug mafia, with the help of Lakshmi plant, was disguising cocaine as salt and shipping it through Allen Manufacturing.'

'Johnson Allen was the owner of Allen Manufacturing,' Forbes intervened.

'Right, sir.'

'Understood, Richard. So, for the past few years, they were making a lot of money. But somehow, Johnson Allen had leaked the information to my informers, and thus, in the past few days, the drug mafia suffered. Allen paid the price for his negligence,' Forbes said. He was glad that he got Richard on the case.

'Yes, sir. However, there is a small correction.'

'What, Richard?' Forbes added.

'Can you tell me the name of your informer?' I said unashamedly.

'Richard,' Forbes shouted. 'You know informers have to be nurtured, and their staple diet is confidentiality.'

'Sir, if I may add that you have no informer,' I said unabashedly.

Forbes literally fell from his executive chair. How could I know that? Forbes did not know how sharp I was. Forbes said in a chaffed voice, 'H... How... I mean what?'

'Let's not keep secrets,' I said firmly.

Forbes got the shock of his life. He never knew that I was such a capable person. Forbes knew about my ability to solve crimes, but the ability to read between lines this sharply he experienced for the first time.

Forbes conceded, 'You are right, Richard.'

'Tell me the truth,' I demanded.

'Some two weeks back, I received a call from a girl and then a report by post. The girl said that there is some process by which cocaine, methamphetamine, heroin, etc., contrabands were disguised as salt.'

'You did not believe it,' I intervened.

'Yes. But I asked Dr. Johnathon to verify. He confirmed that there was a paper published by Prof.

Lakshmi Trust of Edinburgh University. Johnathon told me that there were rumours in the narcotic department a couple of years back that Lakshmi Trust is helping Henry Walter. But with the death of Walter, it died down.'

'Then Dr. Johnathon told you about the Lakshmi plant, its latex, and its flower juice.'

'Yes, Richard. However, it was still in theory when a couple of days back, I received a call from that same girl. She told me that Allen Manufacturing's goods were coming by road. I sent Alex and Dr. Johnathon, and to my surprise, it was really cocaine and not salt.'

'Then you received a call last night,' I added.

'Yes. Around 3 pm, when I thought to involve you instead of Alex alone. I was not sure that the Bungalow No. 9 murder that you are investigating belonged to Johnson Allen, the owner of Allen Manufacturing.'

'So, it is one mysterious girl who is behind the famed and perilous London mafia. She alone has caused them a huge loss,' I said.

'I didn't realise until you said so. She indeed is a brave girl,' Forbes said with a tinge of pride. He was happy that there were such bold citizens.

'Or maybe she is extremely committed to the cause,' I said.

Forbes didn't understand what I wanted to say. But I was sure. This mysterious girl was no ordinary girl. She was determined to destroy the mafia at any cost, and she was not afraid of the consequences. This was personal. 'Hell, hath no fury like a woman scorned,' I immediately thought of that idiom.

'Thanks, sir, it is helpful,' I continued. Please give me a warrant to search and seize illegal material at Allen's warehouse in London.'

'That I will do. However, for Allen Manufacturing's factory in Grangemouth...' Forbes was about to say something when I intervened.

'I know that I have to get it from Tulliallan Castle,' I said and cut the call.

Forbes was pleasantly shocked. Forbes' respect for me as a professional went up many folds. He had never met a sharper and more intelligent detective. He was happy that he had involved me in the matter fast.

I was now clear. Mysterious calls – not only once but many. First, that girl tried to reach out to Forbes. Forbes involved Alex and apprehended the truck. Then she called me. But why – she could have called Forbes. Maybe she was misled by those cigar butts in that bungalow and thought of calling the police station instead. I wasn't sure.

I was there with Watson, and the girl wanted to tell us something. Somehow, we didn't get the clue. Watson was missing. I got more worried about him. Because things were looking dangerous.

My thoughts were disturbed by Alex, who had finished his business and, after much difficulty, had found me. 'Shall we leave?' Alex said.

'Alex, do you know a good sketch artist?'

'Sketch artist.'

'Yes, Alex. I want that girl's sketch to be drawn. Whom I met last night. She is the one who was calling Forbes and me.'

'How are you so sure?' Alex questioned.

'I am not, but somehow I have a premonition.'

Alex was confused; however, he said, 'I know a very fine artist. Marianna - the best in the business.'

'Good, take me to her.'

'Marianna is in London,' Alex said.

'Then let's go back. I guess all our work here is over,' I said.

Alex nodded. We both then hopped in the cigarette boat, and by the touch of dusk, we were back at London port.

Chapter VI

ARREST OF NICHOLAS

Alex and I reached London port, and it was around 8 PM. It was dark, although the London port was lit by artificial lighting. We both came out of the port and headed towards the Astra. Alex had parked it in the parking lot.

However, as soon as we moved towards the parking lot, I jumped on Alex, and we both fell on the ground.

Bang!!!

A bullet was fired, and had I not jumped with Alex, either of us would have been the target of that bullet. I said hurriedly, pointing towards a distantly parked car, 'Orange Ford Fiesta.'

Alex took out his Beretta M 1951, and I took out my Smith & Wesson 10. Before our nemesis could fire another shot, we both fired three rounds. I aimed at the tyres of the Ford Fiesta and in two shots, I got the front driver's tyre, and the third nullified the rear tyre just behind the driver's seat.

Alex instinctively aimed at the driver himself. Alex fired three shots, and it seemed the first shot hit the shoulder, and the gun dropped. Our killer was weaponless. The other two shots scraped through the other shoulder, and we could realise that our enemy was in extreme pain.

He started his Ford Fiesta and tried to run away, but the tyres were flat, and he could not move fast. It was good that the nearby crowd was not hurt due to this exchange of fire. There were many pedestrians even at that hour outside the London port at that open parking lot.

Alex and I hopped into the Astra quickly, and after a short chase, we caught hold of our foe. Alex stopped the car just ahead of the Ford Fiesta, blocking its exit. Alex and I quickly jumped out, and Alex pulled out our adversary, who was behind the wheel of that orange Ford Fiesta, while I was alert with my S&W10 in my hand.

He was bleeding profusely. The bullet had pierced his shoulder, and he was in extreme pain. Alex kicked him hard in the chest, 'What's your name?'

The person coughed. He was in extreme pain, but Alex knew no mercy. I was watching like a standby. Other onlookers were also observing from a distance. The two cops had caught hold of a criminal who had fired at them.

Alex then pressed the bullet hole visible on the shoulder with his boot's toe. The person cried out in agony and pain. He uttered a few words feebly, 'Ni...ch... olas.'

'Nicholas!' Alex shouted.

The person lying on the road nodded, coughing and holding his shoulder to stem the bleeding accelerated by Alex's action.

'Who asked you to harm Richard Carlsen?' Alex shouted.

Nicholas remained mum.

Alex placed the Beretta M 1951 just above the other shoulder and barked, 'I think one bullet in one shoulder is not enough for you. The bullet inside your body needs company.'

Alex was about to shoot when Nicholas said, 'Lisa Ross gave me the contract to kill Richard Carlsen – the Senior Police Inspector.'

'Lisa Ross?' Both Alex and I were shocked.

'Who is Lisa Ross?' I asked, just to be doubly sure.

'Daughter of Sam Ross, Mafia lord...' Nicholas passed out while uttering these words.

I and Alex looked at each other. The fact that Lisa Ross had given Nicholas a contract to kill me seemed unlikely. There were murmurs in the local circles though, that Lisa Ross was now the new face for arms business.

'We need to take him to the hospital,' I said with urgency in my tone.

Both Alex and I then lifted Nicholas, who weighed around 65-70 kg and was approximately five feet 7 inches tall. We settled him in the Astra's rear seat and rushed to London City Hospital.

Alex completed the formalities, and soon Nicholas received the necessary treatment. The operating doctor came out of the operation room and briefed both me and Alex. He said, 'The patient is out of danger. The bullet has been removed. There was a significant blood loss, but he will be alright in a couple of days. Nothing to worry about.'

'That is a great relief, doctor,' I said.

The doctor left, and then I said to Alex, 'We need to bolster security here.'

'If you don't mind, I would say let it be. We are thinly staffed, and right now our priority is to search for Watson. It has been almost twenty hours since his disappearance.'

I didn't like the idea, but I agreed with Alex that at present, our priority was searching for Watson. An ailing Nicholas, who was a contract killer, was not our top concern.

'Let me drop you home. It is quite late,' Alex said.

'Is Marianna still working?' I questioned.

'Marianna works late into the night,' Alex responded.

'Then you better take me to her. I need the sketch of that mysterious girl. That is my first priority.'

'Okay,' Alex said.

Shortly after, we were both cruising past the beautiful roads of this magnificent city, London, and in around thirty minutes of driving, Alex swerved the car into a small alley. Then another turn, and we were in an area where the local crowd was looking like hooligans. I saw many lying here and there, as if they had consumed too much liquor or were on drugs. The place was looking ominous when Alex said, 'You need to get down. We must walk the remaining distance. The lane ahead is too narrow to accommodate Astra.'

I wondered where Alex had brought me. But I followed suit. Alex was leading the way. The people around them were bewildered to see two cops walking past them at that hour. It was around ten at night.

Soon we reached a small building. It was looking old, and the plaster was also falling in place. There were straight iron stairs that Alex climbed, and I followed. We reached the first floor, where there was a small dwelling house.

Alex knocked on the door, and it was taking time to answer. I could see that below the crowd was gathering. It seemed the person staying in this dwelling was popular. The crowd was gathering because they thought the cops were here to arrest that person. I was feeling extremely scared. The hooligan-looking people were gathering in large numbers.

Alex, on the contrary, was quite relaxed. He was not worried about the numbers that were gathering below. He continued stroking the door, and soon it was answered. I saw an old woman—maybe a sexagenarian or septuagenarian—who stared at us. She looked at me and Alex and then gave way. Alex entered, and I followed him.

The lady closed the door. Her room from inside was dark and poorly lit. Alex gestured towards a chair, and I sat in the chair that was available. Alex comfortably seated himself, and the lady sat in the chair nearby. There was no sofa or comfortable settee, but only chairs and a small table in that room.

'Yes, what brought you to Whitechapel?' Lady said.

'We need a sketch to be prepared.' Alex replied.

I was looking at the lady. She was so old, and I didn't think she could see very well. How could she prepare a sketch? I was ruining the fact that I relied on Alex. But I had no option. I had to play ball.

'Hundred pounds.' Lady shouted.

'What are you crazy?' I instantly responded.

'Hundred and five pounds.' Lady said calmly.

'What, is this a joke?' I replied again. I got up from the chair in excitement.

'Hundred and ten pounds.' Lady said again.

'Agreed.' Alex said that before I could say anything. I was shocked.

Alex looked into my eyes and then comforted me.

Alex and I then took out whatever money we had on our person, and it barely totalled to a hundred and ten pounds. We were literally left with no money. Lady took the money, counted it, and then clinched it in her right arm.

Lady got up from her seat and then gestured for us to follow her. I and Alex followed her, and soon we were in the other room. There was a long table with a mattress on it, and then there was strange-looking equipment over that table. It was similar to an instrument that appeared to take brain mapping for a CT scan. Was this lady so rich to afford a complex CT scan machine? I was completely confused. Or was the instrument just a placebo?

'Lie down.' The lady growled.

'I didn't understand.' I said.

'What word did you not understand, lie down.' Lady scoffed.

Alex gestured to me to lie on the table. I lied down without further questions. My head was just near the big donut-shaped equipment; rather, my head was inside, and the rest of my body was lying outside the donut.

The lady then walked towards a small tripod. A big canvas was there. There were many brushes, oil paints, and pencils of varied sizes and paints lying on the tray attached to the tripod.

Lady shouted, 'Who will describe?'

Alex added, 'Richard, she is ready. Please tell her what you have in mind.'

I was surprised. Instead of simply asking me, she was so sarcastic. But I ignored it and went into deep thought about the previous night. I saw that girl, who was around five feet six inches or so; she had small blonde mid-size hair, large eyes, and a beautiful face, which squealed that she may be of Italian descent. Her eyes were blue, and her face was flawless. Her build was normal, and she was neither skinny nor fat.

I started describing what I witnessed, and the old lady started stroking her pencils on the canvas. Soon the lady pressed a button on the tripod, which was connected to the donut-shaped equipment, and I felt as if some small spray hit me. I went into a trance and started explaining to the girl who opened that rose wood door in as many details as I could. Maybe if the spray had not hit, I would not have been in such a trance to explain the minutiae.

The lady soon was asking many questions, and I was responding to them. In no time, the cotton rag on the cotton was filled with a figure, and Alex was looking at that beautiful figurine with intent. The girl drawn by Marianna was beautiful. Marianna drew even the smallest of details, such as a little scar on the right shoulder, the torn shirt there, dishevelled hairs, a scared appearance on the face, torn denim jeans, etc.

What I realised later was that the donut-type machine was also sending some voice signals to Marianna as to at which point my voice tone was more forceful, where I was a little soft. That indicated something to Marianna that may be what I remember clearly and for what I was not that sure of.

In the next thirty minutes, Marianna gave shape to the girl in my mind. Marianna said, 'Come and see.'

I got up from the table and walked toward Marianna. My head was aching, and it felt heavy. The spray had a strange impact on me. I reached the canvas and saw the painting, leaving me utterly shocked.

The girl was just as I had imagined her. It seemed nearly impossible to create such a sketch. It appeared as if the girl could step out of the drawing and start speaking. Marianna had a magical touch. The one hundred and ten pounds were well worth the effort. I kissed Marianna's hand and took the painting.

I rolled it into a scroll and glanced at Alex.

'I told you she was the best,' Alex said with pride.

'She indeed is,' I replied.

'Well, young chaps, my work gets easier with the help of Methamphetamine,' the lady admitted.

I was shocked. She was confessing to using an illegal substance. I didn't say much, but the lady continued, 'The spray was to increase your alertness while keeping you sedated. It makes my work a lot easier.'

I didn't fully understand. This meant that the drug trade had penetrated so deeply that a septuagenarian lady could easily obtain such a drug.

Alex saw my expression and understood my dilemma. He said, 'Richard, let's leave. It's getting late.'

We both thanked the old lady and left her house. There was a huge crowd outside her house, and somehow, I and Alex left, cutting them in between.

Was Marianna a drug peddler? Why were so many hooligans here? I was in my deep thoughts, and I didn't realise that we had walked to where the Astra was parked. Alex and I sat down and left Whitechapel as soon as we could. That was not a safe place for cops in uniform.

It was almost midnight, and the past twenty-four hours were extremely tiresome for me. I reached home, and as usual, Emily opened the door. 'You looked exhausted.' Emily said.

'Yes, it was an adventurous twenty-four hours.'

'What is that scroll in your hand?' Emily enquired.

'It is the painting of the girl whom I met when I went to answer the first mysterious call.' I replied.

Emily took the painting from my hands and opened it. She gave it a good look. She had many expressions. No wife would like her husband meeting girls as beautiful as depicted in that painting. She didn't say much. I also didn't get into any arguments, so I took the painting from her hand and scrolled it back.

'Alex knows this great sketch artist who could make a painting as real as if someone had taken a picture.'

I responded and then went inside the room. I put the painting on the desk and dumped myself on the bed.

I was extremely tired and did not know when I had fallen into deep sleep. I slept in my uniform.

I got up around 7 a.m. I didn't realise it, but at night Emily might have opened my shoes and belt. She had put me in a comfortable pose and draped me in a blanket. I rubbed my eyes and, yawning, got up from my bed.

I saw that the painting scroll was kept on the table where I had put it last night. I was tired and started searching for Emily. I wanted to have a good cup of coffee. Emily was not to be found, but I heard some noise in the kitchen. I presumed it was Emily, so I entered the kitchen and, surprising enough, found Ms. Taylor.

'Good morning.' Ms. Taylor looked at me and said,

'Morning. Where is Emily? I questioned.

'She has gone out this morning.'

'Morning.' I checked the hanging wall clock. It is just 7 a.m. Where Emily had gone that early

'You need a good vegetable soup for lunch; Emily had gone to the supermarket to get the stuff.' Ms. Taylor ended my curiosity.

'Oh. She is a good wife.' I said it with a slight grin. I was extremely lucky to have Emily.

'You want something?' Ms. Taylor asked.

'A cup of coffee.' I said.

'Sure. You just freshen up; I will serve you.' Ms. Taylor responded while she was totally occupied with the kitchen work.

'Am, as for Watson...' I wanted to comfort her.

'Did you get any news?' Ms. Taylor asked. She stopped for a while and looked at me with lots of optimism.

'Not yet. But you don't worry; I will surely find out.' I made a promise.

Ms. Taylor was not interested in such false promises. She got back to the chores she was doing.

I got the signal and left the kitchen. I got ready, and after my usual morning schedule, I was sitting on the sofa in the living room. I was fresh and energetic after a good sleep and shower. I was waiting for the coffee.

In the meantime, I thought of looking at the painting prepared by Marianna. I got the scroll from my room and sat with it on the sofa set. I opened the painting scroll, and with my right hand holding the cotton rag at one end, I made it wide open. I could not help but praise Marianna for making such a live image of that girl. The mysterious girl - was she behind the downfall of the drug mafia in the past few days? Was she the reason why Johnson Allen was killed? I must meet my friend Wordsworth to gather more news about Allen.

Ms. Taylor had prepared the coffee. She had come with two cups of coffee, and she sat beside me. We were both enjoying coffee when Ms. Taylor took a look at the opened painting. She put her cup on the table, took the painting in her hands, and opened it up properly. She saw the girl in the painting and exclaimed.

'Richard, how do you know her?' She questioned.

I was surprised. Did she know about that girl?

'I and Watson met her in bungalow no. 9. She opened the door.' I responded.

'She...' Ms. Taylor said it surprisingly.

'You know her.' I asked.

'No.' Ms. Taylor responded.

I was not sure why Ms. Taylor was looking surprised at that sketch image. However, my question was answered shortly.

'This girl, if I am not mistaken, used to visit Watson for the past two to three days on a regular basis.' Ms. Taylor said this while continuing to stare at the painting.

'What?' I said it shockingly. How was that possible?

She again had a deep look. The painting was made meticulously, and there was no room for doubt or confusion. She said, 'I am sure. It was she.'

'This girl used to meet Watson.' I said this while I was still in shock.

'Yes, around three days ago, she had come to our home also. Then, the day before yesterday, Watson took her on his motorcycle.'

'You asked who she was, right?' I was curious.

'I did. But Watson hushed me and said not to be nosy, like Emily,' Ms. Taylor explained.

I was surprised by this new discovery. If Watson had been meeting this girl, why hadn't he told me? He had seen the girl in that bungalow, but both he and the girl had acted as if they were meeting for the first time. Something didn't add up.

I immediately called Alex. I knew he might be tired and possibly asleep, but to my surprise, he answered the call promptly.

'Yes,' Alex said.

'Can we meet?' I requested.

'I'll come right away,' Alex responded.

'Okay. I'm waiting for you. Come,' I said and ended the call.

I got ready, and soon Alex arrived at my home. I took the painting and left. Emily had not returned, so I informed Ms. Taylor that I might be late. I had to go investigate the case.

Alex and I were soon in Alex's Astra, speeding along the morning roads of this great city, London. Alex asked, 'What happened? You look disturbed.'

'Watson had been meeting this girl regularly in the past two or three days,' I said, holding up the hand that held the painting, folded into a scroll.

'What?' Alex exclaimed in surprise.

'Yes. Despite that, Watson never mentioned that he knew the girl.'

'Do you think Watson was involved?' Alex questioned.

'I'm not sure, but now, when I consider Watson's sudden disappearance and the absence of any signs of struggle at the scene, it suggests that Watson has deliberately disappeared.'

'Don't forget, Watson was the one who killed Henry Walter,' Alex added.

'Yes, the team was led by Louis, but it was Watson who killed Walter. Walter accidentally spilled some highly corrosive acid on his face and body,' I added.

'If we view the situation in this new light and twist the story...'

'That means Watson was working for Sam Ross. He killed Henry Walter, who was the only adversary.

Sam Ross became the sole kingpin of the mafia in London.'

'The girl was behind this mafia. She somehow found out that Watson was involved, and that's why she closed the door. She managed to call you there, but when she saw Watson with you, she got scared.'

'Possible, Alex. But something doesn't add up.'

'What?'

'If Watson was involved, why was the girl meeting him?'

'Maybe the girl initially thought Watson would be of help. She was the one who was the informer. But the mistake she made was relying on Watson,' Alex concluded.

I nodded. The storyline seemed plausible, but I needed more confirmation before I could be certain about it. Lost in thought, I didn't realise that Alex had asked, 'Where to?'

I had forgotten that I hadn't informed Alex about our destination yet. 'I assume Robert might have finished his work. Let's go to the forensic lab,' I said.

Alex promptly drove the car to the forensic lab, which was located near our police station.

I and Alex were sitting in Robert's cabin, and Robert was showing us something on the large television screen.

'The deceased indeed are Johnson Allen and a lady who might be in her mid-sixties.' Robert said.

'How are you so sure about Allen?' I enquired.

'Because the fingerprint all across the house matched that of the deceased. Now it was highly unlikely that someone was in the house, but he was not the owner.'

'That is still a weak piece of evidence.' I countered.

'Then what you suggest—great Carlsen, sir.' Robert said with punity.

'Not sure. But it was also possible that there was another sexagenarian person living in the house for a long time, and he could be deceased.' I concluded.

'Ok.' Robert nodded. But then he added, 'How will you counter this fact that the person who died had the same blood group as registered for Johnson Allen?' Robert showed a medical report for Johnson Allen, which the team found in the file in the house.

'I will still say that what if someone was staying in that house as Johnson Allen?' I tried to counter.

'Then you are right.' Robert conceded.

'Richard, but we have no proof that Johnson Allen was not staying in that house.' Alex countered.

'I met the security guard of bungalow no. 10, and he suggested that Johnson Allen rarely come into the house. Some caretakers used to come. What if the fingerprints and the body belong to that caretaker?' I expressed my doubt.

'That is possible, Mr. Carlsen.' Robert accepted.

'What else do you have? What about that lady?' I questioned.

'I found some fingerprints of that lady too. Her hair and blood traces were there. That means the lady was in the house for at least a couple of days.' Robert added.

'Interestingly. We don't have any clue about her.' I said.

'More so, the lady used to touch the strange plant you said more often than the man.' Robert added.

'What?' I said, shocked.

'Yes, I found traces of the plant under the woman's fingernails but not on the body of the deceased man.' Robert said. He opened some pictures on the screen.

'That means the lady was using the Lakshmi plant to help camouflage the drugs,' Alex said.

'Could that mean she was Prof. Lakshmi Trust?' I said, shocked.

'But why would they kill her? I can understand about Allen. Allen stupidly leaked out the secret to that girl. But why will the mafia kill Lakshmi Trust,' Alex added.

'I am not sure,' I said. Then I asked, looking at Robert, 'Robert, is it possible for you to check the record and see whether the deceased lady can be Prof. Lakshmi Trust?'

'I have already done that,' Robert said.

'How come? We never told you about Lakshmi Trust,' I was surprised.

'Dr. Johnathon had told me earlier about Lakshmi Trust and that Lakshmi plant. I had called him up when I was researching about it.'

'You are extremely sharp, Robert,' I said, praising Robert.

'Thanks. But I am afraid, whatever public domain information we have, it is not enough to conclude that the deceased was Prof. Lakshmi Trust. But the good part is ...'

I intervened before Robert could complete, 'there is no evidence that suggests otherwise.'

'Yes,' Robert laughed and nodded.

'Could you check whether Watson's fingerprints are there?' I questioned.

'I will. Watson's print might be there in our records from the past,' Robert said.

'Also, how many fingerprints were there?' I asked.

'There seemed to be seven people,' Robert said.

'Seven?' I questioned.

'One is of the lady, as you were saying, whom you met. I found a few strands of hair belonging to a young girl. Though there was one more set of strands of hair belonging to another lady, maybe in her early thirties.'

'What?' I said, shocked.

'Yes, sir,' Robert said.

'This means there were two dead bodies – the sexagenarian people, then two ladies, one whom I might have met and one more, and there were three more people there,' I said.

'It could be the two security guards and Watson,' Alex added.

'Seems so,' I said.

'I will check about Watson and confirm shortly,' Robert said.

'If you get to know anything else, let me know,' I told Robert and left the room. Alex followed me.

One thing was clear: the person who died could be Johnson Allen and Lakshmi Trust, or it could be some caretaker who used to visit and Lakshmi Trust, or some other combination. The case was getting mired in deep secrecies, and every tryst added a new layer. I need to act fast.

We both hopped into Alex's Astra.

'Where to?' Alex asked.

'Let's first go to the Registrar's office,' I concluded.

Chapter VII

DRUG MAFIA

Alex then drove the car to Croydon. It was around an hour's drive from the forensic lab, and soon we were on our way.

'What will we do there?' Alex questioned.

'Nothing much. I just wanted to know whether Bungalow no. 9 is indeed in the name of Johnson Allen,' I said.

'Okay. But we already know that,' Alex said.

'Yes, but not from any official source. We are just conjecturing based on people's statements,' I said.

'Agreed.' Alex nodded.

'More so, my friend Wordsworth also stays there. I will better meet him and get some more information about Johnson Allen and Allen Manufacturing.'

'Who is Wordsworth?' Alex questioned.

'He is an expert who knows a lot about the corporate world. He is a lawyer by qualification but now advises people on where to invest. I distinctly remember he had advised people not to invest in Allen Manufacturing, but that bet had gone wrong.'

'Oh. Then he might have done a deep study,' Alex said sarcastically.

'Yes, his bet had gone wrong. Rarely he commits such folly. I want to understand his perspective.'

'Okay.'

Alex started concentrating on the driving. I was just piecing the information together. A mysterious call came, and I was invited to Bungalow no. 9. The girl didn't know that I would bring Watson with me. She saw Watson, got scared, and closed the door. She was the girl who was meeting Watson in the past few days. As she might have thought the one who killed Henry Walter would be of help. But there she made a mistake. Watson was a stooge for Sam Ross. He captured her and kept her in that bungalow.

Johanson Allen, Sam Ross, Watson, all were hand in gloves. Still, the girl managed to call me there. Allen and Lakshmi were killed by Sam Ross. But why? Difficult to answer now.

And Watson? How did he get involved in this? This was a big shock. I was not clear about where this investigation was headed. I needed help.

We soon reached the Croydon – HM Land Registry office.

We both were sitting in the Assistant Registrar's office. It was around ten o'clock in the morning, and the Registrar's office was as expected – bustling with activities. The Assistant Registrar was sitting in his usual comfy chair, while I and Alex were sitting just opposite. The thick register containing the details of various bungalows and plots registered with the HM Land Registry office in Croydon was lying in front of us. The relevant page with the details of Bungalow No. 9 in the Notting Hill area was what I and Alex were currently examining. We had read it quite a few times.

'Can we get a copy of this page?' I said politely.

The young man, who appeared to be in his mid to late-twenties, got up with the thick register and went inside. The room was filled with various staff members, each busy with their usual duties. The Assistant Registrar returned with a copy and handed it to me.

'Can you please sign and write that it is a true copy,' I insisted.

'Sure, Mr. Carlsen,' the Assistant Manager responded and did the necessary. He handed over the stamped copy with his own signature to me. I gave that copy to Alex. The Assistant Registrar was about to close the main register when I insisted, 'One minute. Can I have another look?'

The Assistant Registrar hesitated; however, I didn't wait for his response. I opened the relevant page and started reading the information. I shouted, 'Alex, can you confirm whatever I say with the copy that we have just received.'

Alex nodded and took the photocopied page in his hand. The Assistant Registrar was looking at me.

'I need to be sure that whatever you have given me as a true copy is indeed what is written in this main register,' I said peevishly.

'Mr. Carlsen, I made the photocopy of this exact file,' the Assistant Registrar protested. Though his voice was meek, I ignored it.

Others in the office were now looking at the cabin of the Assistant Registrar. It was a glass cabin, and thus, whatever was going on was visible to the other workers and staff outside. They were used to police people coming to the office, but this time they had guessed that something was different.

I started reading the details aloud.

'Title Number: HL34597'

'Right,' Alex said.

'Address – Bungalow No. 9, Notting Hill Area, London, HU53HT,' I said.

'Right,' Alex said again.

'Registered Owner – Mr. Johnson Allen'

'Yes'

'Other Covenants – Nominee – none;

Owner's date of birth – 23rd June 1914;

Date of Purchase – 2nd July 1977;

Purchase Amount – 186,000 GBP'

'Right' Alex said, though now he had a tinge of boredom. He was not sure about what I was up to.

'Owner's will extract – Post the death of the owner the aforesaid property bearing title number HL34597 will be automatically mutated to Mr. Boris Allen – caretaker of the property.'

'That is what it states in the copy also,' Alex said.

'Thanks,' I looked at the Assistant Registrar who had hitherto looked tense but now appeared relieved.

Alex folded the paper, and the Assistant Registrar was about to close the file when I said, 'Just one small thing.'

The Assistant Registrar looked at me.

'Are you sure that the contents matched?' I asked the Assistant Registrar.

He started trembling. Alex was confused.

It was at that time I peeled off the transparent tape that was covering the covenant paragraph. Beneath the tape was a rectangular slip superimposed on the main register page. Now, with the removal of the tape and the added slip, the covenant portion read differently. I read it aloud,

'Post the death of the owner the aforesaid property bearing title number HL34597 will be escheated to the State.'

Alex was shocked to see this. Someone had craftily placed a piece of paper and transparent tape so that on plain reading, it appeared that the death of Johnson Allen would result in Boris Allen getting the property worth £186,000.

'I am extremely sorry. I desperately needed money. My wife is terminally ill,' Assistant Registrar pleaded.

'That's alright. I ain't going to use it,' I said, holding the copy in which he had signed as a true copy and had forged content.

'Who asked you to do that?' Alex shouted.

'Some unknown person. He gave me a huge sum and made me do this a few days ago.'

'When?' I asked.

'Precisely on 5th October,' Assistant Registrar said.

'You remember the date so well,' Alex questioned.

'It is the date when my wife's operation was due. The person paid the money, with which I could manage the operation.'

'Can you describe the person?' I asked.

The Assistant Registrar described the person, and with the vague description he provided, I could match him with the second security guard I met at Bungalow no. 9.

'If anyone approaches you, remember to call Baker Street police station,' I warned him.

'Sure, sir,' Assistant Registrar said. Then he added, 'One Mr. Louis had come yesterday, and he had taken a copy of the same, though without my signature.'

'That is alright. He would give it to us only,' I said.

'That is the difference between Richard Carlsen and others. He can see what others can't,' Alex added.

We both left the room and got into the car.

'Where next?' Alex asked.

'Wordsworth's house in South Croydon,' I said.

Alex started the car in that direction.

'How did you realise that there was some tape?' Alex asked.

'When I was reading the covenant, the lad's facial expression was changing. I realised something was fishy. I concentrated hard and found a slight swell where the tape was,' I said.

'And that was enough for the great Carlsen,' Alex said and laughed.

I laughed too.

Soon we reached Wordsworth's house and were sitting with him in his living room. Wordsworth was a man in his late forties, tall and overweight. His large paunch indicated he had little interest in exercise.

'What brought the great Carlsen to this humble abode?' Wordsworth said, revealing his yellowed teeth.

Alex didn't understand why I brought him here. He couldn't see the value that this overweight man could add. What Alex didn't know was that Wordsworth had made a lot of money advising his clients on various companies. He was a general corporate lawyer but had transitioned into an investment adviser. His recommendations had often yielded significant dividends, except for Allen Manufacturing. That had been a disaster.

'I just wanted to know that a couple of years ago, you advised on Allen Manufacturing,' I said.

'Don't remind me of that mess,' Wordsworth growled.

'No, I want to know how you analysed it so wrongly,' I added.

'My analysis wasn't wrong. That damn Johnson Allen had shady connections.'

'Shady connections?' I was confused.

'He was associated with the Mafia,' Wordsworth said with clear irritation.

'I'm not sure what you mean,' I said.

'He was on the verge of bankruptcy but then suddenly bounced back,' Wordsworth said. He got up and went to make a glass of his preferred whisky. He didn't offer us any, but helped himself to a gulp.

Alex was already disliking this man but didn't voice his thoughts. Wordsworth was not known for his courtesy or hospitality.

'Can you elaborate?' I asked.

'Why are you so interested?' Wordsworth questioned while sipping on his whisky, standing at some distance from the couches where we were sitting.

'He was murdered in his bungalow. I am investigating that,' I said.

'That was bound to happen. Sam Ross is not an easy customer to deal with,' Wordsworth said with a hint of contempt.

'Please help me understand more about him. I know you have studied his business thoroughly,' I pleaded.

'Alright, my dear friend, for old times' sake,' Wordsworth said.

Alex wondered how I had become friends with this questionable character. What Alex didn't know was that I and Wordsworth had previously worked together on a financial scam, which I had cracked with his help and financial acumen.

'Around five years back, Johnson Allen's salt business was at its prime. He was making a lot of money. However, then the competition got the better of him, and slowly his prime slid.'

'And around two years back, he was on the verge of bankruptcy.' I have heard that from you on various occasions.

'Yes. I predicted that around three years back after a detailed study.' Wordsworth said while finishing his whisky. His tone was now revealing his inebriated state. He continued, 'I short-sale huge amounts of Allen Manufacturing stock, which means I was bearish on it. My clients also did the same on my advice. I wrote a piece explaining how Allen Manufacturing's business was unsustainable. Soon it would be a victim of hostile takeover from its competitors. The shares were tumbling, and I was about to make a huge profit alongside many of my clients.'

'Then the turnaround happened. Allen Manufacturing survived the downfall,' I added.

'Yes, Richard. Suddenly, Johnson Allen got a huge amount of money and he himself started purchasing shares. That sudden boost in share purchases by the owner himself gave stability to the stock. Slowly, he managed to reverse the trend. The salt sales were beyond comprehension,' Wordsworth said, gritting his teeth.

'But how is it established that he is associated with the mafia?' I asked, still confused.

'Rumours say so,' Wordsworth said.

Alex was flabbergasted. We had come here just to hear what rumours say. These would have no weight in a court of law.

'Wordsworth, please, help me,' I pleaded.

'Alright, Richard. Let me share some data,' Wordsworth said. He went inside to his room and brought a thick file. He gave the file to me. It was titled 'Allen Manufacturing Report 1979 to 1981.'

'You can go through this in detail for hard proof,' Wordsworth said.

I was flipping through the pages to understand, but to my untrained financial mind, it was not clear how these numbers established that Johnson Allen was associated with Sam Ross.

Wordsworth sensed my confusion. He added, 'The total production of Allen Manufacturing in 1979 was 50 million metric tonnes. How much was the sales?'

I was struggling with the numbers, and Wordsworth understood. He continued, 'Sales were merely 20 million tonnes, and even that could be an exaggeration. Almost 40 percent unsold.'

I then saw those numbers and understood what Wordsworth was saying.

'Now, suppose you are the owner of this company, which had almost 30 million metric tonnes of stock in trade. What would be your next step?'

'I would not produce next year. I would first try to sell what I have,' I said instinctively.

'That was exceptional. You hit the nail, Richard,' Wordsworth said.

I wasn't sure what he was saying.

'Now check the production for the next year,' Wordsworth said.

I checked the numbers, and my eyes widened.

'60 million metric tonnes,' Wordsworth said.

'What do you make of it?' Alex intervened.

'That these were not salt. These were camouflaged drugs sold in the black market. To cover this huge quantity of drugs, they manufactured huge quantities of salt despite little sales of their product,' I explained.

'And that's why in the 1980s, Johnson Allen got so much money to purchase his own stock,' I further added.

'You are a sharp guy, Richard,' Wordsworth said.

I now understood the game. By showing simple numbers available in the public domain, Wordsworth had made a shocking revelation. Allen Manufacturing's sales had been dwindling, but the production numbers were high. Why? The answer was simple: these were drugs sold through drug dealers. The quantity of salt over the years reduced to a mere 25 to 30 percent, and the rest were drugs sold in the market. That's why he made a lot of money.

Now it was clear that Johnson Allen, along with Sam Ross, was involved in the drug business, and that's why he was murdered.

I spent some more time with Wordsworth to understand the file completely. I thanked him. He had helped me a lot, and soon I and Alex were in the Astra on the streets of London.

'That was helpful. I thought that ugly-looking fatso would be of no help. But he indeed was,' Alex said.

'Yes, he had always been sharp with numbers,' I added.

'This reminded me that to complete the story you must meet one more important person,' Alex said.

'Who?' I asked.

'Dominik Kirk,' Alex said.

'What, but he is in London Central Prison.'

'All the better, you know where he is.'

'He was an erstwhile drug dealer. How can he be of help?' I questioned.

'He was and still is more than a drug peddler. He can do stuff which otherwise is unfathomable for people.' Alex said with conviction. He continued, 'You must meet him. He knows the ins and outs of the mafia. What's more, he is a good friend of mine, and he knows you well too.'

'If you so insist, let's meet him,' I said.

Alex then took the car towards London Central prison. Today was the day when we were meeting various people: Robert, the forensic guy; the Assistant Registrar; Wordsworth; and now Dominik Kirk. The best part was that in these meetings, I was getting a clear picture of the entire series of events that had been happening over the past few years. It was clear that the drug mafia was now in the sole control of Sam Ross. Johnson Allen was his ally, but because of Allen's leakage of information, he was punished with a brutal death. Watson may be involved too.

I need to nab these culprits soon. Sam Ross had been out of sight for the past period, and I was not sure how I would catch hold of him. But if Sam Ross was behind this, I need to bring him to justice. I have vowed to myself that I would catch hold of the criminals and liberate that mysterious girl. She had single-handedly taken on the drug mafia, and now, as a watchdog of this city, it's my abundant duty to protect her and bring the criminals to their knees.

I didn't realise in my thoughts when we reached the central prison. Alex completed the formalities, and soon we were in a big hall. We were waiting for Dominik Kirk. It was around half past one pm, and mostly it was the time for post-lunch rest for prisoners. The local rules permitted visitors between four to five pm. However, Alex had a good rapport with both the Jailer and Dominik Kirk, so we were fortunate to have the audience at that hour.

We were sitting inside a large room where visitors were generally allowed to meet the inmates. As there was no one, the room appeared extremely large to us. We waited for around ten minutes or so when a person entered. He was large-built, stout, with broad shoulders and bluish eyes. Even in his fifties, he was fit and strong. The little paunch suited his giant stride. He sat beside us after a customary glance at Alex, to which he nodded to indicate that he remembered him well.

'Hi Dominik,' Alex said.

'Hi, Cop,' Dominik responded with his baritone.

'Hope you remember me,' Alex said.

'Well, I don't forget my friends,' Dominik said. With a pause, he added, 'Foes, never.'

'Haha,' Alex laughed a bit. 'You still haven't forgotten who was behind your arrest.'

'How can I when the cop who arrested me has not forgotten?' Dominik replied with a grin.

I was confused. Alex had apprehended Dominik. Why would he help Alex? I was absolutely confused. Alex sensed that, and he replied, 'Richard, Dominik was arrested by me, but by that time, Dominik had become a changed man. He was an efficient player in the drug markets, and in his heyday, he was one of the bigger names, if not the biggest.'

'So, he was working with Henry Walter?' I asked.

'Working with,' Alex smirked. 'Dominik gave run for the money to both Walter and Ross. If he had continued on that path, he would either have been dead or the kingpin of the London mafia,' Alex added.

Dominik was listening with intent to the discussions between the two cops.

'I presume he had a change of heart,' I said, though there was no conviction in my voice.

'Love,' Dominik intervened. 'The famous Richard Carlsen will not understand. But love is the most lethal commodity.'

I was surprised that Dominik knew about me.

'Everyone knows the great Carlsen,' Dominik said. It seemed he had read my mind.

'Dominik lost his wife in the police chase. She was a simple girl and wanted a peaceful life. Ironically, she died when Dominik had decided to surrender,' Alex added.

Dominik went into some thoughts. They were painful, as could be gathered from his demeanour.

'Life is cruel,' I said, mostly to comfort our jailed friend.

'Dominik's wife had taken a promise from him before she died that he would lead a peaceful life. Dominik surrendered, and I helped him get as little a sentence as possible. He is now serving a ten-year term,' Alex said.

'Oh,' I exclaimed.

'What brought you here?' Dominik asked. He didn't want to discuss his personal life much, so he wanted to get on with the main discussion. Moreover, he had limited time on hand.

'We are here to understand the drug mafia. We are confused as of now,' Alex said.

'That is no surprise. London police could never fathom what was going on with the London mafia. Otherwise, they could have finished them early,' Dominik sarcastically said.

'Dominik,' I said with utmost seriousness, 'I received a call last night that a gruesome crime was to happen in Bungalow No. 9. Watson and I reached there. I met a girl.'

I showed Dominik the sketch that Marianna had drawn.

I continued further, 'This girl, in a brief discussion, closed the door, and I felt that something was fishy. I asked Watson to guard and went to make a call to Forbes to get a search warrant for that bungalow. When I returned, Watson was missing, and the guard changed. The new guard didn't let me in, but when I forced him, he did allow me in, but then he disappeared too. I believe they all ran in a BMW e-21 car. When I forced myself inside the bungalow, I found two deceased: an old man and an old lady.'

'To whom did the bungalow belong?' Dominik questioned in between.

'Johnson Allen – owner of Allen Manufacturing Co. - the salt company,' I responded.

'I got what you want to know,' Dominik said.

'Really,' I was surprised.

'Yes, but before I jump the gun, you complete what you want to tell,' Dominik said.

'We then received a call that Customs had seized a boat belonging to Carlson Marine and Transport Co. which was carrying salt from Allen Manufacturing from Grangemouth Port to London Port.'

'That salt was disguised cocaine or methamphetamine or at best heroin,' Dominik said with a smirk.

'Yes, it was cocaine,' I replied.

'As expected, please continue.' Dominik said.

'There was another such consignment. What I could find was that there was a girl who was tipping Forbes with this information. So, I have framed a theory,' I said.

'Interesting; You have some theory. I am all ears.' Dominik said.

'Henry Walter and Sam Ross were mafia lords. Somehow there was an unwritten rule between the two that Walter would do drugs and Ross would do illegal arms. But Watson killed Walter in an encounter. Ross was now the whole and sole. He met Lakshmi Trust, whom Henry Walter was using to convert drugs into powdered sugar or salt. Ross then joined hands with Allen, and they both became drug lords.'

'Interesting. Carlsen, in the past twenty-four hours, you have gathered the information that many cops struggled to collect for months. But what was your theory?' Dominik said.

'My theory is simple. Henry Walter's daughter,' I said, pointing to the girl in that sketch, 'she wanted to take revenge. She somehow followed them and then gave this news to Forbes. She then met Watson as she thought Watson would help her nab Sam Ross. There, she committed a mistake. She fell prey to Sam Ross. I want to save her now and arrest these culprits,' I said.

'Interesting, Mr. Carlsen. You indeed are the sharpest that the London police has,' Dominik said.

'He is the celebrated *Hawk-eye* accoladed inspector,' Alex added.

Dominik smiled and nodded.

'But let me say there are flaws.' Dominik said.

'What?' Alex exclaimed.

'I know,' I added. I looked at Alex and gestured for him to calm down. 'If the girl was in the custody of Sam Ross last night, then who gave the tip about the two boats? She can't give that tip,' I said with a tinge of sadness.

'Yes,' Dominik said.

'Also, who was the sexagenarian lady whose dead body we found?' I asked, although the question was aimed at myself.

'Right,' Dominik said. 'I cannot answer those questions. But you must know something. That will help.'

'That's why we are here. Please guide us.' I said politely.

'The London mafia till 1975 to 1977 was easily divided into two big wings: Henry Walter and Sam Ross. But they both were doing everything. Walter was doing well, but Ross too was not behind either,' Dominik said and got up from his chair. He went to the windowsill and continued from there.

'Around 1977-78, Sam Ross discovered Alfa Combat's source in Czech and got a huge consignment from there. It was sold as a hot cake in the market. Sam Ross became big and powerful. Around the same time, Walter got his hands on Lakshmi Trust.'

'So, both the mafia lords have something to boast about,' I said.

'That is what people and police know. But the fact is that both have a super boss.'

'What?' Alex and I both came in shock.

'Yes, those rumours that you have heard are not rumours but true.'

Alex and I got up from our chairs and went near Dominik.

'This third person, many say, is a cop, and many say a beautiful girl who had mesmerised both Walter and Ross.'

A police person. I was thinking deeply, and there was a premonition. But I didn't utter a word.

'You are thinking right, Richard. It could be...' Dominik said.

'Watson,' I said before Dominik could complete.

'Yes. Because Watson killed Walter when he could have arrested him easily. Walter was surrounded. There is a strong feeling in our mafia circle that Watson wanted to kill that day,' Dominik added.

I was shocked. I never realised that Watson could do that. How come I could not figure that out? Watson's lifestyle was simple. Why would he? Why?

'Because Watson was a capable man, and London police failed him,' Dominik responded.

'What?' I was shocked.

'Yes, Richard. Watson always got the raw deal from the force. He was never given any accolade, and thus he became a fat, unscrupulous officer. He was extremely capable, but Forbes never considered him. That day, Louis led the mission when Watson was far more capable.'

I never realised this. Watson had that heartburn. He indeed was smart, but he was never given his due. Alex,

Louis, all were now sub-inspectors, I was a Senior Police Inspector, but Watson, despite killing the mafia lord Henry Walter, was a mere Head Constable. Was Watson wanting revenge against the police department?

'Moreso, if this kingpin is not Watson, then it would be someone so influential that even Watson could not do much,' Dominik said.

I was wondering who that far more powerful person was. A girl, as Dominik was alleging, seemed unlikely. A cop was a strong possibility. Was any other police person involved with the London mafia?

It was when a constable came and politely said, 'The meeting time is over. Dominik must return to his cell.'

Dominik obeyed and left the room. I and Alex were watching him. The meeting got over so abruptly. However, Dominik returned within a short while and holding the door shouted, 'I guess you must meet the daughter of Henry Walter. Sarah Walter. She is studying chemistry at Edinburgh University. Her botany is also good. She will be helpful.'

Dominik left. But I was in shock. I thought that the girl whom I met that day in Bungalow was Henry Walter's daughter. If Sarah Walter was studying in Edinburgh, Scotland, who was that mysterious girl? With every passing moment, the controversy was getting deeper and deeper.

I need to meet Sarah Taylor.

We both left the prison after thanking the jailer. Meeting with Dominik Kirk was helpful. I was now aware much about the mafia. However, the thought of that kingpin was troubling me.

Chapter VIII

VISIT TO GRANGEMOUTH

'Alex, we need to go to Grangemouth,' I said.

'What?' Alex was confused.

'Yes. First, we will collect the warrants from the Commissioner's office and then we will move to Grangemouth. Let's visit Allen Manufacturing Co.'

Alex was perplexed, but he played ball. Soon, we went to the Commissioner's office, got the warrants, and ate whatever we could in the canteen there. I called home, and Emily had returned by that time. I told her that I am going to visit Allen Manufacturing Co. Emily protested, but by now, she was used to my stubbornness.

Emily didn't know that Watson was involved. She would, for sure, tell Ms. Taylor, and if Ms. Taylor was in my house just to keep an eye on me, she would tell Watson about my visit to Allen Manufacturing. I would come to know about the truth then.

Even Alex was not aware of my complete plan. I had now prepared to end this mafia game. Sam Ross was operating from some hideout. Nicholas had confessed that the attack on me was at the behest of Lisa Ross. This meant that Lisa Ross was fully involved with her father.

I also need to meet Sarah Walter, and if she was not the same girl as that of the painting, then who was she? I need to find out about that mysterious girl also.

It was around ten at night when Alex and I embarked upon the long journey to Grangemouth. Alex was a fabulous driver, though I was a touch better, and I knew we would reach Grangemouth by morning dawn. I had time for a quick nap, and I offered Alex to drive halfway in case he would like to rest. He was a stud and decided that he would rest while we returned, if required. He could manage without sleep for many days he had always boasted. Now was the time to test it.

The thoughts of this complex case kept running on a replay mode. The mysterious call, meeting a girl in that bungalow, whether it was the same girl or not was still a mystery. Then the chain of events, guards disappeared, Watson disappeared, a huge consignment of salt at London port, and all leading to the involvement of Watson in killing Henry Walter so as to help Sam Ross. Dominik Kirk believed that there was another kingpin. Who this person could be? Johnson Allen was killed because he leaked info to that informer girl who caused huge losses to the mafia. All these thoughts clouded my mind, and I didn't realise when I slept. The beautiful flowing breeze through the Astra's windowpane also helped. I was in deep slumber shortly.

Soon, the beautiful rays of mild sunlight hit me and woke me up. We were almost entering Grangemouth.

Alex had realised that I had woken up. 'We shall soon reach Livingston. What is the plan?' Alex asked.

'We are not going to Livingston. Take the car to Falkirk,' I replied.

'What? Falkirk?' Alex questioned.

'Carlson Marine and Transport's office is in Falkirk,' I said with intent.

'But what will we get going to the boat owner's office?' Alex questioned.

'You know that the two boats hired by Allen Manufacturing belonged to Carlson Marine,' I replied.

'But isn't that obvious? Both companies are in Grangemouth,' Alex was still perplexed.

'That is. However, when you are involved in such dubious trades, you would not hire boats as well as trucks of the same company.' I responded, with a glint in my eye.

Alex did not understand much, but he swirled the wheel in his hands, and soon we were on our way to Falkirk. It was around seven in the morning, and the blue hour was at its last leg. The Carlson Marine and Transport office was large, and I could estimate that it would be around a hundred and fifty square metres. The three-storey building was sprawling and covered most of the area. Sufficient space was available for the movement of vehicles, including large trucks. The guard at the gate was alert at that hour and stopped both of us outside.

The guard looked at both of us perplexed. The two London police officials in their uniform got down from the official Vauxhall Astra and walked towards him. He did not know what to do. He said politely, 'Yes, whom would you like to meet, sirs.'

'The owner of this company.' I said in a stern voice.

'The office opens at 9,' the guard said. He was still completely cautious. It seemed unlikely that the morning guard, who was completing the night shift, was so alert. It meant that he had just arrived, and that meant there was someone important in the office. I deduced.

'We will wait inside. I guess there might be some waiting room,' I insisted.

'Sirs, I am extremely sorry,' the guard replied. He firmly clenched the butt of the rifle that was hanging on his right shoulder. I could guess from his body language that he was ready for a fight.

'What if I say we have a warrant to search and seize?' I said firmly.

The guard calmed down a bit and was confused. He said, 'Can you show me the warrant, Sir.'

'For sure.' I said.

I looked at Alex, and before the guard could have understood anything, Alex handed him a well-placed strike to the vagal nerve in the neck, and the guard passed out immediately. Though the guard wouldn't remain unconscious for long, but that much time was enough for us to confine him with rope and gag his mouth with our handkerchief. We threw him behind the thick grass, and Alex took the keys that were attached to his belt.

We opened the door and went inside. It was a huge place, and after around 150 feet of walking, we were at the main office door. Before we would enter, I took a quick look at the back of the building. I saw some plantations, and if I was not mistaken, I saw the same trumpets and flowers, signifying it to be a Lakshmi plant.

I looked at Alex and whispered, 'My suspicion was right. This Andrew Carlson, the owner of this company, is hand in gloves with the mafia.'

'How are you so sure?' Alex questioned.

I pointed towards the plantation behind the huge building. Alex had a peep, but he was still confused.

We both entered the main gate. It was not locked, and there was no one on the ground floor. The guard was right. The office would open at 9 am, and thus no one was there at that hour. We were cautious, and with our respective Smith & Wesson Model 10 and Beretta M1951 pistols in our hands, we slowly combed the office. It was a usual marine and transport office. I had seen a truck and a small boat also lying outside.

We heard some voices, and I gestured to Alex that it was coming from the second floor. We cautiously moved towards the second floor and saw that the middle room, which displayed the signboard '*Andrew Carlson - MD & CEO*,' had two people. The lights were on, and they were discussing something, though the voices were not clear. The wooden door had a glass window from where we had a quick glimpse. Fortunately for us, the two people were too engrossed in talking to each other; they didn't notice our presence.

I pointed towards Alex, and in a seamless manner, Alex kicked the door open, and we both were inside.

'Hands up,' I shouted.

The person who was sitting facing us, in the main executive chair, stood up with hands in the air. I could guess he was Andrew Carlson. His guest, who had his back towards us, also slowly got up.

'Turn!' I shouted to that person.

However, before we could understand, the other person kicked his chair with wheels, which hit me and Alex fiercely, and we tumbled down. Before we could act, in a lightning-fast manner, the other guy jumped out of the window from the second floor. I followed him and peeped from the window. I saw that the person had fallen safely on the ground using the overhanging eave at the edge of the floor protruding outwards. He was no mean person but a trained guy who could jump from the second floor unharmed. He got up and ran towards the back of the building, from where we could not see him anymore through that window.

Alex thought of chasing him, but I gestured him to wait. I and Alex both then went near the guy who was still standing at the other side of the long table.

'What's your name?' I growled.

'An... Andrew Carlson,' the person said while gulping his saliva.

'I guessed so,' I said.

'Can I put my hands down?' He requested.

He was a fat guy with his belly protruding so much that I never thought he could be of any danger to us. I nodded, and the person put his hands down and sighed in relief.

'Who was that guy?' I asked.

Andrew didn't answer and was still thinking.

'Sam Ross,' Alex intervened.

Andrew was shocked. 'How do you know?' He instinctively asked Alex.

'Wild guess.' Alex said.

I was not sure whether it was good of Alex to hint the answer to Andrew. I wanted Andrew to answer on his own about that person. Nonetheless, I asked, 'Why was that mafia lord in your cabin at this hour.'

Andrew knew he was cornered and had not much to hide. He had to tell the truth.

'I am not into any wrongdoing. I simply give my boats and trucks on hire,' the fat guy said.

I gestured Alex, and he reached the other side of the table. Before Andrew could understand anything, Alex gave him a tight slap. The slap was so hard that there was a slight cut on the lips.

Andrew cried in pain.

'Listen, you fatso,' I barked. 'We are capable of inflicting extreme pain that your fat body could not handle. We are short of time. The more you delay, the more painful it will be for you.'

Andrew was nursing his lips. When Alex gave him another blow, this time with the pistol butt, Andrew fell to the ground.

The cut became deeper, and the blood started oozing out.

Andrew shouted, 'Wait, please don't hurt me. I will tell everything.'

Alex extended his hand, and Andrew got up. We made him sit back in his chair.

'I was working with Allen Manufacturing for the past four or so years. Around two years back, Sam Ross summoned me to the Allen Manufacturing office, where he told me that I have to take the salts and transport them into various places in London, Birmingham, Edinburgh, Glasgow, etc. I used to provide my trucks for hire.'

'You have a Lakshmi plant in your backyard, in your office. Can you explain that?' I growled.

Andrew got up from his chair and started walking. He said, 'I was asked by Sam Ross to grow these plants here. If they were grown in Allen Manufacturing's office, someday they would get caught. Though the main place was my farmland, where I grew this plantation.'

'Why was Sam Ross here?' Alex questioned.

'In the past few days, my trucks got caught by the London police, and then Sam Ross wanted me to ship through boats. I got the whiff that someday I would be in trouble because, for the first time in the past two years, the trucks were caught.'

'You then tried to blackmail Sam Ross,' I questioned.

'Well, kind of. I did not send the full quantities in boats. There were four boats hired, but I sent only two. The other stuff I shipped with my own transport. I also sent a third cigarette boat to keep an eye on these boat shipments. And as usual, the first boat was caught by customs, and thus I had to ask my people to leave the boat and run away.'

Andrew didn't realise it, but while walking, he was now standing at the window from which Sam Ross had jumped and run away. It was a risky place, and if someone wanted, he could shoot this fat guy from outside. Sam Ross was still outside there.

Before we could ask anything further, Bang!!!

There was a shot from outside. The aim was so accurate that the bullet pierced Andrew Carlson's heart, and he fell to the floor. Alex went to the window and saw that Sam Ross had fired the shot from his car. The guard whom we had sedated was also sitting in that car. Alex fired back, but Sam Ross ran away.

'I could tell you a big secret... ' Andrew said while clutching his heart. He was shocked by the treachery of Sam Ross. I knew that Andrew was hiding something big, but now he wanted to disclose.

'Yes, Andrew.' I said, lowering my ear to his mouth.

'Aa, the drug mafia – Sam no, Henry... but em...,' Andrew died before he could say anything further.

I was shocked. I did not know what to do. This was not our jurisdiction. The local police could arrive at any time, and things could get worse. We had no permission from Tulliallan Castle. It was the name for the Scotland police headquarters where the highest authority, the Chief Constable of Police of Scotland, sat.

I gestured to Alex, and we both ran away from that place and soon were in the Astra.

'Let's visit Livingston,' I said.

Alex had driven the car to Livingston. The factory of Allen Manufacturing was vast, resembling any other salt factory. It was nearly eight in the morning, and we expected the factory to have already started its operations. The guard stood outside, spotting the two uniformed police personnel approaching him.

'Sir, how can I help you?' the guard politely inquired.

'We're here to visit the factory and meet the owner.'

'Are you investigating the death of our owner?' the guard asked.

'Yes,' I responded.

'Well, Sir, please give me a minute,' the guard said politely.

He then dialled the intercom, and soon a person emerged from the factory's main gate. He was of Indian origin, thin, tall, and slightly dark-complexioned, in his mid-thirties. He politely introduced himself, 'I am Vijay, the manager of this factory. Please come in,' he said and led us through the main door. We walked for about a hundred feet until we reached the main administrative building.

'Would you like to have coffee or something?' Vijay offered.

'No thanks. I would like to have a tour of the factory,' I replied.

'Very well,' Vijay agreed.

Vijay then took us inside; it was another five to seven minutes' walk when we reached the huge factory. 'This is the place where evaporated salt is produced.' Vijay said. He was more than cooperative and did not ask for any warrants, etc. That surprised me. He was coming across as he wanted to help us investigate the death of his company's owner.

He showed us a huge place and said, 'At this place the sea water is stored.'

He then took us a few metres ahead. He continued, 'The water recycled from the evaporated process is pumped into the salt deposit. Then the water dissolves the salt to form saturated brine in the cavern.'

Vijay showed us the cavern on the map that was displayed there. It showed the process of Evaporation Salt Manufacturing.

'The resulting brine is forced back to the surface by pressure created by water entering the cavern.' Vijay said to show the map.

I and Alex were looking with complete concentration. I was trying to find whatever I could.

'The brine is then boiled using steam, which causes water to evaporate and crystals to form. After which, the salt is centrifuged, dried, cooled, screened, and packed for distribution to customers.' Vijay said.

He showed us all these places physically as well. I found nothing unusual, either in the factory or in the process. Rather, I found it mesmerising that everything was so clean.

'What are the shifts?' I asked.

'We have only one shift, from 9 am to 5 pm. People will start arriving shortly,' Vijay replied.

'Why are you here so early in the office then?' I inquired.

'I had to clean the factory, and last night, we had some people clean it.'

'You cleaned the factory in the middle of the week?' I asked suspiciously.

'We don't follow any specific pattern and clean whenever required. The cleaning has just been completed, which is why I am in the office,' Vijay explained calmly.

'So, you produce only through one method?' I questioned.

'No, we also use the rock salt production method, where we do underground mining.'

'Then you might have explosives and corrosives too,' I noted.

'We do have highly corrosive acids and explosives,' Vijay confirmed.

I nodded.

'Do you want me to take you there?' Vijay offered.

'Yes, I wouldn't mind a full tour,' I accepted.

Vijay then led me to the area where rock salt production was carried out. It was the second oldest method of producing salt - underground mining. This was probably the most dramatic method of gathering salt. Large machines traversed vast cave-like passageways, performing various operations.

Accompanied by Vijay and Alex, I descended into the shaft. I could see there were two shafts, one for humans and one for materials. At that time, there were no activities, but I gathered that the operation of undercutting was done first. Large machines cut a slot of around ten feet in depth across the bottom of the solid salt wall. Then, on the smooth floor, salt was picked up after blasting.

I did not find anything unusual. What I did not understand was how, in this complex scenario, they would convert drugs into powdered sugar with the help of the latex of the Lakshmi plant. Then I asked Vijay, 'You use the huge corrosive acid for what purposes?'

'Well, for the same things, we use the explosives,' Vijay replied.

'But explosives would be handier than acid,' I pointed out.

'True. That's why we don't use acid much,' Vijay responded.

What Vijay was not aware of was that I could spot things that others generally missed.

'How much do you produce?' I suddenly asked.

Vijay was surprised. It took him some time to make a calculation.

'You are the manager of this factory, and you don't know your total production,' Alex teased.

'Well, it's around ten million metric tonnes,' Vijay eventually said.

'How many factories does Allen Manufacturing have?' I asked.

'We had quite a few in the past, but at present, I'm not sure how many of them still exist,' Vijay admitted, showing his lack of knowledge on this subject.

'Do you know your sales figures?' I inquired.

'Not much. Our role is to produce and send it to various warehouses across Britain,' Vijay replied.

I then conducted a quick scan of the entire factory, hopping here and there, with Alex following me. After about twenty to twenty-five minutes of scanning the factory, I couldn't find anything unusual.

'Thanks, Vijay. You were extremely helpful. If we need anything, I'll get in touch with you.' I expressed my gratitude.

'Sure, Officer.' Vijay replied.

Alex and I left the factory.

'There was no sign of the Lakshmi plant at the factory. I'm confused. Where did they use to camouflage the drugs?' Alex asked as he drove the car.

'I can now understand the entire game.' I remarked.

'What?' Alex inquired.

'Yes, Alex. Allen Manufacturing is the one where they would camouflage drugs.' I stated.

'What? How could you say that?' Alex questioned.

'I'll answer all your questions, but first, take us to the University of Edinburgh.' I requested.

'Okay, Sir,' Alex nodded and drove the car towards Edinburgh.

Edinburgh was approximately thirty minutes away from Livingston.

'I'm dying to learn.' Alex commented.

'It was simple. Andrew Carlson, the owner of Carlson Marine & Transport, Johnson Allen, the owner of Allen Manufacturing, Sam Ross, the mafia lord, they were all in this together. Allen Manufacturing would produce substantial quantities of salt and camouflage drugs as salt. Then they would mix them and transport them through Carlson's trucks across Britain.' I explained.

'But we didn't see any place in the factory where they would camouflage drugs. There was no Lakshmi plant.' Alex pointed out.

'My dear Alex, we saw it with our own eyes. The difference is that you didn't register it.' I said somewhat condescendingly.

'What?' Alex was bewildered.

'The second method - rock salt mining - was nothing but a facade. It's the place where they would camouflage drugs with powdered sugar or salt.' I clarified.

'How are you so sure?' Alex asked.

'Because there isn't any rock salt mining in Scotland. There can't be,' I asserted.

Alex was looking absolutely confused.

'Dear Alex, rock salt can be mined where there are huge deposits of rock salt. Otherwise, commercially, it will make no sense. Despite negligible rock salt, a bankrupt company like Allen Manufacturing, which two years ago invested in this facility itself, indicated that there was something fishy. I read the report carefully that Wordsworth had given.'

Alex was now completely surprised. He had an expression of awe on his face. He did not know how a cop could be so extremely sharp.

I ignored his fanboy moment and continued. 'So, Allen Manufacturing would get the Lakshmi plant from the huge plantation of Andrew, as he said before dying, and then use this rock salt production facility for camouflaging drugs.'

'Then they would send it across through Andrew Carlson.' Alex added.

'Yes, in this way, they all had control over the process, and thus it was an equal trade. Everyone's skin in the game.' I added.

'That was brilliant.' Alex said.

'Yes Alex. That's why people like Marianna were in a position to get drugs that easily. Under the London police's nose, the drugs were being sold as salt, and we could not get a sniff of them.'

'Unless the girl called Forbes.'

'Yes, now that mysterious girl changed the game within a matter of a few weeks.' I added.

I went into deep thought about who she was. I opened the painting and gazed at that beautiful girl. Her torn shirt, one leg with a sandal, one barefoot, holding the door slightly ajar, her denim jeans with some scratches. That girl had the courage to bring the entire drug mafia down to its knees. I needed to find her quickly.

I didn't realise that we had reached the University of Edinburgh. After some small formalities, we could enter the vast, sprawling university campus. The huge hundred- and thirty-five-acre campus had various disciplines and departments, and soon we were at the botany department. We parked the car in the designated area and walked towards the classes.

It was around eleven in the morning, and I could guess the classes might have gone over. There were a lot of students rushing here and there, and I could see some professors and teachers rushing too. We two were standing confused as to where to start when a voice engaged us: 'Can I help you, officers?' A middle-aged man said

'Hi, I am Richard Carlsen. Senior Police Inspector, London Police.' I said this while extending my hand for a handshake.

'Hi, I am Professor Zod Halliday from the Plant Science department. How can I help you, officer?

'I am looking for a student, Sarah Taylor, in the Plant Science department. Can you tell me where I can go and find her? I said.

'Well, she is my teaching assistant. Come, I will take you to her. She is still in her class.' Halliday said this and started walking towards a classroom.

I was surprised. Today seemed to be a lucky day. Alex and I followed Prof. Halliday, and soon we were in a room where only one girl was sitting and doing some work. She got disturbed looking at two approaching police personnel in uniform and Prof. Halliday.

'Sarah, these two officers' were looking for you.' Halliday said.

'Hi.' Sarah said. She got up from her seat. Though she was not looking frightened or cautioned by our presence, I had a good look at her. She was in her mid- to late-twenties, a girl of medium height. She had bluish eyes and was dressed neatly in a frock. She definitely was not that girl whom I met at the bungalow.

'Hi Sarah. I am Richard Carlsen.'

'The famous cop of the London police.' Sarah said it excitedly.

'You have heard about me.' I was surprised.

'Yes. Who has not? She retorted.

'I am surprised.' I said.

'Don't be. You might know that I am the daughter of the deceased Henry Walter. My father was not in the cleanest of businesses. So, I used to hear about police people. You were quite famous amongst them.' Sarah said.

I see she had no discomfort talking about her father or his death. I was surprised at his unusually cool behaviour for such a young girl. I was expecting her to hide, run, not meet us, or otherwise not be cooperative with us. She, on the contrary, was forthcoming.

'Well, I wanted to discuss something with you.' I said.

'We can go to the nearby shop in King's building. It has wonderful coffee. I guess you can offer me a coffee.' Sarah said.

'Yes, why not? My pleasure, young lady.' I said.

'I can come with you.' Halliday said.

'I can handle them. They don't look like causing any harm to me.' Sarah said.

She got up, took her things, and started moving. I and Alex followed her. Halliday bowed and left for his own business.

Soon we were sitting and sipping coffee when I asked Sarah, 'Can you tell us about your childhood and parents?'

'My mum died while giving birth to me.'

Both Alex and I said, 'Sorry to learn...'

'My father took good care of me. I was very close to him, and he would do anything for me. My childhood was good, though at times we had to shift places and my father would be missing for many days.' Sarah said. She had no shame in accepting that her father was a mafia lord.

'I then joined this college, and my father died.' Sarah said it with a blank face.

'I can understand that would mean a tremendous loss for you.' I said.

'Yes, I lost my entire world that day. I hate that Watson - he brutally and wantonly killed my father. He could have arrested him instead.' Sarah said it with bitterness.

'How do you know Watson could have arrested him?' I asked.

'Well, I also have well-wishers. My father has been killed, not all his men.' Sarah replied curtly.

'But...' I wanted to ask something when Sarah interrupted.

'If you want to talk about my father and his death, I am sorry. I'm not game for it.' She got up and started walking away.

'Sarah, listen, we will talk about something else!' I shouted.

She came back and sat in her seat. There were other students too, but they were at some distance, so we could talk easily with Sarah.

'Tell me about your University of Edinburgh life and journey,' I asked.

'I joined them around four years back as a B.Sc. Plant Science student.'

'Interesting,' I said, while finishing my coffee.

'I, along with being a regular student from my second year onwards, became a teaching assistant. I joined Professor Lakshmi Trust as her assistant. That gave me some money.'

'What? Lakshmi Trust?' Alex said.

'Do you know her?' Sarah asked.

'No, we don't know her. The name looks familiar to Alex,' I intervened without looking at Alex.

Alex got the cue and said, 'Well, I have not heard such a name before; it looked weird.'

'Her mother was Indian, married to a British. So, her mother named her Lakshmi, and she took the surname of her British father,' Sarah explained.

'So, you were with her for how long?' I asked.

'For around two years. I was helping her with her research on some Narcissus genus plant,' Sarah said.

'Okay then. What happened?' I asked.

'She disappeared. There were rumours that Sam Ross and his stooges kidnapped her. Though I am not sure whether the rumour was right or not,' Sarah said unabashedly.

I was looking at her body language. She was looking extremely comfortable. She had no qualms disclosing sensitive information about her father and even her role with Lakshmi Trust. With Alex's sudden reaction, I was sure she had gathered that we knew about the discovery of Lakshmi Trust.

'Are you aware of the details of her research? Whether she could complete it?' I asked.

'Well, in the meantime, my father got killed. I was shocked. So, I left her in between. I took a break from studying. Then, after a few months, I joined back. It was then when Prof. Halliday helped me, and after that, I have not heard or met Prof. Lakshmi Trust,' Sarah responded.

'But post your father's death, were you in financial crisis?' Alex asked.

Though looking at her dress, shoes, etc., I didn't see her in any financial crisis.

'Well, actually not. My father had kept a lot of property for me, and more so, I used to get paid for my teaching assistantship. So, I never found myself short of money. It is enough for my needs,' Sarah responded.

'Anything else that you think we should know?' I asked.

'Well, nothing specific. However, since you asked about Prof. Lakshmi Trust, you should know that Lisa Ross was her favourite,' Sarah said, looking left and right.

'What? Lisa Ross,' I asked.

'Yes, the daughter of mafia lord Sam Ross,' Sarah said with affront.

'Was she also a Plant Science student here?' I asked.

'No, she was a chemistry student here. However, she was extremely close to Prof. Trust. When my father died, I had taken a break. At that time, I am told that she was the one helping Prof. Trust. But then both of them disappeared.'

'Both disappeared together?' I questioned.

'No. First Prof. Lakshmi Trust disappeared. Lisa Ross was a student here, and she continued. But then, around a few months back, she also disappeared. There is a rumour that she somehow did not gel well with her father now,' Sarah said.

'She didn't gel with her father. How could you say so?' I asked.

Sarah got up from her seat and started walking away. 'I told you whatever I know. I have to rush as I have another important class to attend.'

She didn't wait for any response from our side and left the coffee shop, and we could do nothing but see her going away.

Both Alex and I were not sure whether Sarah had helped us or confused us with whatever she had told us. As per her, Lisa Ross was involved with Lakshmi Trust, but Lisa Ross now had sour relations with her own father. Something was not adding up.

'What's next, Chief?' Alex queried.

'I have a hunch. I want to confirm it. Arrange a meeting with the Director of Student Systems and Administration Directorate of the university,' I said.

Soon, we were sitting in the office of Carry Godfrey, the Director of Student Systems and Administration Directorate. We had already requested that we wanted to see the student details of Lisa Ross as we were investigating multiple murders at Bungalow no. 9 of Notting Hill Area, and it seemed Lisa Ross was there at that time.

Godfrey had a large register before him and he opened it up for us. He was a person in his late fifties with bald hair and exceptionally fair skin. His tender hands opened the register, and soon we were looking at the details of Lisa Ross.

My premonition was right. Lisa Ross was the same girl as the painting. I unrolled the painting scroll and presented it before Godfrey.

'Mr. Godfrey, can you confirm she is Lisa Ross?' I asked.

Godfrey nodded in a moment. The painting made by Marianna was so clear that it looked like a photograph rather than a sketch. Godfrey understood that there was something wrong.

'I met this girl two days back at the crime scene, before the offence was committed. Can you tell me whatever you know about her?'

Godfrey nodded and settled back in his leather chair. Alex and I were waiting for his response. He slowly settled down and said, 'Well, Lisa Ross indeed is the girl in that sketch. She joined us around two years back as an MSc Medicinal and Biological Chemistry postgraduate student.'

Both Alex and I were listening with full intent. Alex was making notes in his diary too. It was getting too much for him to remember just based on his memory.

'She then was helping Prof. Lakshmi Trust in her research,' I asked in between.

'Who told you? It is rubbish,' Godfrey said.

'Then?' I asked.

'She hardly used to meet Prof. Trust. She was pursuing her course. It was a one-year course, but by the time she could finish the course, Sarah attacked Lisa Ross.'

'What? Sarah attacked Lisa?' I was shocked.

'Yes. Sarah's father was killed in a police encounter. However, Sarah blamed Lisa's father. However, we cautioned her and threatened her with rustication,' Godfrey said.

'That is something usual.' I said.

'Yes, but after that incident, Lisa and Sarah never had any issue.'

'But I heard that Lisa went missing for the past few months,' I queried.

'Yes, Inspector. Lisa finished her course, but then she suddenly disappeared after that. We wanted to have her also as a teaching assistant, but she was nowhere to be found,' Godfrey said.

'Since when was she missing?' I questioned.

'Around a year back,' Godfrey replied.

I was making some mental notes.

'Lisa Ross and her parents, what was their relationship. Do you have any idea?' I asked.

'The relationship between Lisa Ross and her parents was normal. They had divorced long ago, and Lisa's mother had shifted to the US by marrying some businessman there. Lisa stayed with her father. However, just before she went missing, there was a rumour that she was telling everyone her father was not his usual self. Something was amiss about him.'

'Can I have pictures of Lisa Ross and Sarah Taylor both?' I said.

'Yes, sure. I will get it arranged,' Godfrey said.

We thanked him and came out of his cabin. We thought of meeting Sarah again, but she was not to be found. We asked about her hostel and went there. She was not there. After meeting us, she had disappeared.

Chapter IX

THE PLOT THICKENS

Alex and I headed back to London. It was a good sunny day, and the drive back was a pleasure. Alex stopped for refuelling, and we both had a quick bite. Then we started back. Alex said while driving on the main carriageway.

'This is quite complex.'

'Don't flinch, dear. I can see it clearly now.'

'What? Then can you show me your vision too. Great Carlsen,' Alex said mockingly.

'It is simple and crystal clear, my friend,' I said while lighting my favourite Havana cigar and getting intoxicated by the puff.

My monologue started.

'This story begins in 1977 when London Mafia had two main groups. One led by Sam Ross and the other by Henry Walter. Both were in constant one-upmanship; however, Sam Ross got the upper hand when he managed to get Alfa Combat from the Czechs. That was selling like hotcakes in the market, and it was so craftly marketed that everyone wanted to have that beauty of a pistol.'

'So, in 1977 or around, Sam Ross became the clear leader,' Alex intervened.

'Yes, kind of,' I said.

'Ok,' Alex nodded. He was attempting to learn the complex puzzle.

'So, for the next year or so until 1979, Sam Ross was the clear leader. And maybe was getting closer to that third mysterious person. The real mafia kingpin,' I said.

'Ok,' Alex nodded.

'But this was the time when Sarah Walter met Lakshmi Trust, and she came to know about the research she was working on. Sarah told this to her father. Henry Walter then, with the help of Lakshmi Trust, started camouflaging drugs as powdered sugar. But they needed someone who has an established distribution channel.'

'This is where Johnson Allen was required,' Alex said.

'Yes. Johnson Allen was on the verge of bankruptcy. He needed help. Henry Walter and he joined hands. Walter grew in stature,' I added.

'At that time, Sam Ross with the help of Watson killed Henry Walter,' Alex said.

'Yes, maybe Sam Ross was closer to Andrew Carlson. Whose help Johnson Allen took to send goods. Andrew Carlson squealed to Sam Ross, who with the help of Watson ensured Walter was silenced,' I explained.

'This is how Sam Ross became the ultimate Mafia lord,' Alex added.

'Yes. However, one thing is not clear: whether it was Sarah Walter who was the informer or if it was Lisa Ross. Why was Lisa Ross there in that bungalow that day? Why was she in touch with Watson?' I said.

'Do you think Watson was that third person – the Kingpin?' Alex questioned.

'I believe Watson may be involved, and maybe his wife also knew about it, but I doubt whether Watson could be that third person,' I said.

'Why?'

'Because if Watson was the Kingpin, he would not be involved in such day-to-day activities. It was extremely risky for a mafia lord to expose himself to such things. Seems counterintuitive,' I said.

'This means there is someone else. Some extremely powerful cop,' Alex said.

'Or some lady,' I said.

'Lady,' Alex questioned.

'Maybe the lady whose body we found,' I said.

'But if she was the kingpin – the super boss - who killed her,' Alex asked.

'That's where I am stuck,' I said.

'What about Watson then?' Alex questioned.

'Watson would work for both Sam Ross and Henry Walter. He was agnostic. Whoever paid him more was his man. Maybe he got more money from Ross or maybe that super-boss forced Watson, and he killed Walter.'

'So, if I have understood you right, by 1978-79, Sam Ross was leading the show, when Henry Walter's daughter met Prof. Lakshmi Trust. She told her father, and he abducted Lakshmi Trust, forced her, and then, with the help of Johnson Allen, became successful and powerful by selling drugs. Obviously, the drug market would fetch more than Alfa Combat. In no time, Henry Walter became the obvious leader. At that time, Andrew Carlson and Sam Ross planned to kill Walter and, with the help of Watson, did it. Sam Ross then took over the drugs mafia too and became super powerful,' Alex repeated what we discussed.

'Yes, but even Sam Ross had not been seen in the past two years by people. He was operating from a hideout. It seemed, from what Godfrey, the University Student Director, said that even Lisa Ross was not meeting him regularly,' I added.

'But Ms. Watson helped you identify Watson meeting Lisa Ross. Why would she do that if she was involved?' Alex questioned.

'That is true. It is confusing me. But when I deliberately told that I am going to Allen Manufacturing, you see Vijay was there at night and he cleaned the factory,' I said.

'But still could not mislead the great Carlsen,' Alex said.

'Haha. Thanks. I deliberately told Emily because I knew that the news would get to Ms. Taylor and through her to Watson, and that's why Vijay, the manager, seemed prepared as if he was expecting us.'

'But you met Lisa at that Bungalow. You think that Sam Ross is so cruel that he would harm his own daughter?' Alex questioned.

'That is a puzzle which I am not able to solve. Lisa called me at that bungalow. She was the informer of Forbes and was in touch with Watson. However, when Lisa saw Watson with me, she got confused and closed the door.'

'But why would she not tell you then and there everything?'

'Maybe she thought that I am with Watson,' I conjectured.

'Or maybe she thought you would come with a police team, and when she saw only you two were there, she got circumspect.'

'That may be right, Alex. I guessed that was the reason why she closed the door in a jiffy.'

Alex and I were discussing the case and slowly discussed all the angles once again. After some time, to give Alex some rest, I took over the driving. He slept for a while. We drove almost non-stop, except at a petrol bunk for refuelling and getting a quick bite. We reached London by nightfall of that Friday night.

It was late at night, and we reached home. I was greeted by Emily. Alex left so that he could also get some sleep after a gruelling day.

'It was an extremely tiring day for you. How was it in Scotland?' Emily questioned.

She was concerned and prepared something to eat. I saw Ms. Taylor also helping Emily in the preparation of the food.

I sat at the dining table, and soon a sandwich with red wine was served. Emily and Ms. Taylor sat beside me at the table too. Ms. Taylor asked in a feeble voice, 'Any news of Watson.'

'Not yet, Ms. Taylor. But I have gathered that he is not in trouble. He is alright,' I said.

'What? How are you so sure,' Ms. Taylor questioned.

'I cannot tell you in full detail, but please note that Watson is absolutely okay. He will soon be meeting you,' I said assuredly.

'Good. If Richard is saying so, please be comforted that Watson is ok,' Emily said while holding hands with Ms. Taylor.

I quickly finished my dinner and was about to retyre when Robert called me. He was such a workaholic that he would not end his day until the work was over. Emily picked up the call and handed over the phone to me.

'Yes, Robert,' I said.

'You were right. Watson's fingerprints matched inside the house,' Robert said.

'Ok. I guessed so. Thanks,' I said and ended the call.

Emily was standing near me, with Ms. Taylor also nearby.

'What was Robert saying?' Emily questioned.

'Nothing much. Routine,' I said.

I left the two ladies and went inside the room. I took a quick shower, freshened up, and was about to sleep when Emily slept beside me.

'You look extremely troubled. You can share with me,' Emily said.

'Emily, I am afraid, but Ms. Taylor needs to be arrested tomorrow morning.'

'Are you out of your mind,' Emily said in shock. She stood up and sat on the bed.

'Watson was involved in the murder,' I said.

'Are you serious... Watson,' Emily replied. She was literally sitting next to me on the bed while I was lying on the bed.

'He was working for the mafia.'

'But how can you be so sure, Richard? Ms. Taylor is an extremely emotional person.'

'I know. But she too inadvertently helped Watson.'

'But how are you so sure she is helping Watson.'

'Emily, only you knew that I am going to Scotland.'

'Yes.'

'Did you share it with anyone,' I asked.

'Only with Ms. Taylor when we were discussing lunch. I said you wouldn't be coming as you are going to Scotland.'

'Right, and then when I visited Allen Manufacturing, it was clean as a whistle,' I said.

'You mean to say Ms. Taylor told Watson, and he in turn told someone to clear the manufacturing facility in Scotland.'

'Yes, Emily.'

'But why do you think there is something wrong in Allen Manufacturing.'

'I don't think anything is wrong there. Just my premonition.'

'Come on, Richard. You cannot be arresting people based on your stupid premonitions,' Emily said with firmness and lay down on the bed.

'That's why I have not arrested her yet.'

'But I don't understand, when you did not find anything in Allen Manufacturing, what is your hypothesis.'

'At present, I am confused,' I said.

'Then...'

'Emily, I am extremely tired,' I said, cutting her off.

'Ok. We will discuss in the morning,' Emily said.

She kissed me, and we both slept. I was tired and didn't realise when I was in deep slumber.

In the morning, I got ready. I found that Emily and Ms. Taylor were their usual selves. Emily had not discussed with Ms. Taylor. That's what I expected too. I knew Emily would not speak to her.

I kissed Emily said bye to Ms. Taylor and called Alex to my home. Alex and I left the house and went straight to the London City Hospital. The morning was busy in the hospital, though Nicholas had been well attended, it seemed. There was a doctor and a few nurses tending to him.

What I found interesting was that Nicholas had recovered quickly from the deep bullet wound. It had not even been forty-eight hours since the brutal wound, but it seemed that with the padding and gauges all around his shoulders, he was looking comfortable.

'Hi. I hope you are doing well.' I said to him:

'Yes,' Nicholas said with a neutral voice.

He didn't try to escape, even though it was quite possible, as there was hardly any security in the hospital, which seemed disturbing to me. I couldn't understand why a serial killer like him would let himself remain in custody. Why was it so?

'You said that Lisa Ross gave you the contract,' I said.

Nicholas gave me and Alex a deep look, and he nodded. His facial demeanour indicated that he didn't want to entertain questions on those lines, but I wasn't about to relent.

I continued.

'Take a look at these two pictures and identify Lisa Ross for me.' I showed him the pictures of Sarah Walter and Lisa Ross that I obtained from the University of Edinburgh.

'I was told that Lisa Ross wants you killed. I was contacted by a guy. He got my number from an old client of mine,' Nicholas said uninterestingly.

'Can you describe the guy for me,' I said. Alex took out his notebook and pen to note the description.

Nicholas went into deep thought and then said, 'Medium height, a scar on his face that looked like a knife wound after healing, neither too fat nor too thin, well-built, and neatly dressed.'

The description matched the second security guard. I understood that the second security guard, whom I encountered, was deeply involved and an important member of that gang. The previous security guard was a novice.

'When did this person approached you?' I queried.

'Just few hours before I attacked you first at the commissioner office lane.' Nicholas said without any remorse.

I was making a mental note. That meant just after the escapade at Bungalow no. 9 that night the mafia asked that hoax security guard to meet Nicholas and planned an attack on me. They did not want me to be on this case.

'Did you receive the full payment?' Alex questioned.

'No,' Nicholas said.

He got up slowly from the bed and started walking a bit. He was in a separate room, and at present, there were only the three of us. The nurses had left the room. He slowly walked, nursing his damaged shoulder, and limped to the window. He looked outside the second floor at the hustle and bustle of the city.

'Then how were you supposed to get the payment?' Alex continued.

'Well, I was paid five grand, and the remaining fifteen grand I had to get from someone in Edinburgh,' Nicholas said while staring outside the window.

'So you would go to Scotland to receive the payment,' Alex inquired.

'Well, if I was successful in killing a London police inspector, it would be nigh impossible for me to stay in London. I needed the shelter of Scotland, and thus the arrangement. Things would have gotten too hot to handle here,' Nicholas said in a neutral tone.

'Okay. Can you give me the address from where you were supposed to get the payment,' I interjected for the first time in the dialogue between the two.

'15 Polwarth Crescent, Polwarth, Edinburgh.' Nicholas said.

I was shocked that Nicholas was so cooperative. I wasn't sure whether it was part of the plan or if he was genuinely helping us.

I and Alex left Nicholas in the room and went straight to the doctor.

'Can we take Nicholas with us? We need to shift him to police custody,' I said hurriedly.

'Officer, it would be too risky. It looks like the wound is not causing any trouble apparently, but the wound is fresh, and I would suggest waiting for at least another two days before you decide to move him outside medical supervision,' the doctor said.

'Okay,' I nodded and left the doctor's cabin.

Alex and I were now out of the London City Hospital. The hustle and bustle of daily life could be seen writ large and the road outside the hospital was extremely busy, full of life. I looked up at the floor where Nicholas was admitted, though I could see only the hospital building from a glance and said to Alex, 'Alex, beef up the security. Something is telling me Nicholas will escape soon,'

'Okay. I will tell Louis immediately,' Alex said.

I nodded. Then took measured steps towards the Astra that was parked nearby. I and Alex got into the car.

'Take me to Forbes,' I demanded.

Soon, Alex and I went to Forbes' office and were sitting in his cabin shortly.

'Sir, I need an arrest warrant to arrest Ms. Taylor,' I said.

'What? Are you out of your mind,' Forbes said.

'Sir, there is no other way to force Watson.'

'What do you mean?'

'Sir, I have only one lead now, an address: 15 Polwarth Crescent, Polwarth, Edinburgh.'

'That is out of bounds for us,' Forbes said.

'I know. That's why someone has clearly chosen that place. They knew that to raid that house, we need permission from Tulliallan Castle,' I said.

'What is your plan?' Forbes asked.

'Sir, two-fold. Arrest Ms. Taylor and put pressure on Watson to touch base with us.'

'And...' Forbes said while lighting a Havana Cigar.

'Second is that I and Alex will go to this Polwarth address and catch hold of the people there.'

'That is extremely risky,' Forbes said.

'I know, but I have no other option.'

'Okay. I will issue the arrest warrant for Ms. Taylor. Hopefully, you are not troubling an innocent civilian,' Forbes said.

'I know, sir. But desperate times require desperate measures,' I replied.

Forbes nodded and engulfed himself in the cloud of cigar smoke. He, like me, was fond of Havana cigars.

I and Alex left the office. Alex had called Louis to collect the warrant and arrest Ms. Taylor. Also, Alex had told Louis to beef up the security of the London City Hospital.

'Where to,' Alex asked.

'Let's meet Robert one more time,' I said.

'Okay,' Alex nodded.

Soon, we were at the Forensic Lab of Robert. We were sitting in his cabin, and Robert was as usual up to the mark. He was a workaholic, and I had never seen a more committed guy.

'I had already confirmed to you about Watson,' Robert said.

'Yes,' I nodded.

'Now I can confirm about Ms. Lakshmi too,' Robert said.

'What?' I said, surprised.

'Yes,' Robert said.

'Last time it was tentative,' I said.

'Yes. But now I can with reasonable certainty.'

'How?'

'I found from our database that she was arrested in 1980, and her fingerprints were there.'

'She was arrested. For what?' I questioned.

'For attempting to sell drugs to students.'

'What?'

'But I went to the University of Edinburgh; nobody told me this,' I said.

'Well, it was in some school in Livingston,' Robert said.

'Livingston, Scotland' I said.

Robert nodded.

I was making some mental notes. Allen Manufacturing factory where I met Vijay was also in Livingston. Robert continued.

'Though the police could not confirm whether it was drugs, and finally, the court gave her bail.'

'She might have been trying to test whether drugs could be camouflaged as powdered sugar.' I intervened.

'I am not sure about that, but when I cross-checked the fingerprints, now I can say for sure Lakshmi Trust is dead,' Robert concluded.

'Good. Any other lead?'

'Yes.'

I waited expectantly for Robert to speak.

'The Havana cigar butt we got from the house was just a placebo.'

'I am not sure what that means,' I said.

'It meant it was a red herring.'

'Please explain,' I said. I am not clear about the convoluted language and its meaning that Robert was alluding to.

'Those were kept there to mislead. None of the people smoked.'

'How are you so sure?'

'Because when I looked at the butt carefully, they all were not smoked at that time. They were smoked at least a day or two before the murder.'

'So what?' Alex asked.

'But they were all lying in the living room,' Robert said.

'Check whether they were these cigars,' I said and gave my Havana Cigar packet.

'Yes, this brand only,' Robert said.

'Hmm,' I said.

'So, these were kept to mislead,' Alex said.

'Or maybe there was a message in this,' I said.

'Message?' Robert and Alex questioned.

'Yes. These cigars are either consumed by me or by Forbes. So is it that Lisa Ross was giving a message. She knew that the police would definitely comb this place and would get these cigar butts.'

'But how does it help?'

'Does it indicate that I or Forbes are involved or whether it is a message for Forbes or me,' I said, though my tone was not convincing.

'Lisa Ross put these consumed cigar butts of yours and Forbes' brand,' Alex said. He was not convinced enough.

'I am not sure, Alex. Just a wild thought,' I said.

'But you may be right. Otherwise, these cigar butts don't make any sense there. The girl had thrown them in the lobby. But for what purpose.'

'To tell the investigating officer that Forbes or I was involved,' I said.

'Or maybe there was someone else who wanted to give you a message. Maybe a challenge.'

'I am not sure what you mean.' I said.

'They knew Lisa had called the police station. They might have guessed she had dialled you. So this was a challenge for you,' Robert said.

'Watson knew very well that I consume only this brand of cigar,' I said.

'So maybe Watson is throwing a challenge at you,' Alex said.

I was unclear.

'There is one more thing that you should know,' Robert said.

'What?'

'There were seven people as we got seven different fingerprints,' Robert said.

'You told me this last time. Two deceased, two security guards, Lisa Ross, Sam Ross, Watson,' I said.

'Only change is that Sam Ross's fingerprints did not match,' Robert said.

'What?'

'Yes, however surprising it may sound, but Sam Ross was not there,' Robert said.

'That is strange,' I said.

'And...' Robert was about to say something.

'You found the fingerprints matching the deceased Henry Walter,' I said.

'Yes,' Robert said.

Alex was flabbergasted.

Chapter X

THE DISHEVELED LADY

I was back at my police station when Louis came to me.

'We are leaving to arrest Ms. Taylor,' Louis said.

'You are already very late,' I objected.

'Yes, sir. But I wanted you to meet one person,' Louis said.

'Who?' I questioned.

'The caretaker,' Louis said.

Louis then pressed the bell, and a constable came with a middle-aged person, maybe in his late forties to early fifties, bald hair, and a tired face. He seemed to be a person with very little energy. Had he been consuming drugs all his life? His eyes couldn't catch a glimpse properly. He walked haphazardly and reached near my desk.

'He is Boris Allen,' Louis said.

'Okay,' I said.

'As per the registry document, the property would go to him post the death of Johnson Allen,' Louis said with pride.

I had a small grin.

'Good job, Louis. Now you go and get Ms. Taylor. She is at my house. Leave Mr. Boris Allen in my good company,' I said.

'Thanks, sir,' Louis said and left the room.

I gestured Boris to sit down in the chair in front of me. My cabin was larger than the usual inspectors' cabin, and even I have a sofa set. However, I preferred to sit and interact at my table.

'So, are you related to the late Johnson Allen?' I asked.

'Yes, sir,' Boris said in a dull voice. He was not interested in the questioning.

'Where do you stay?'

'Edinburgh.'

'How often do you come here?'

'Whenever Mr. Johnson Allen would ask. He would pay me fifty bucks for each visit.'

'And generally, what were your instructions?'

'Nothing much,' Boris said. He was trembling. It seemed he was an extreme drug addict. Johnson Allen used to give him drugs in addition to the small change.

'Still, what was that – nothing much?' I insisted.

'To take care of the Daffodil plants, the four floors....'

'There are no Daffodils there,' I intervened.

'Sir, there are a few at the back.'

'Okay. You used to water them.'

'Yes, sir. Also, whatever the learned lady would tell me, I would trim them.'

'Learned lady?' I questioned.

He seemed lost. I took the file and opened the page where I had kept a picture of Ms. Lakshmi Trust. I showed him the picture and asked,

'Is she the learned lady?'

'Yes, sir,' Boris responded, though he was sweating and trembling badly.

I knew I could not question him much in this state. I pressed a button, and a constable came.

'Do we have the seized boat and the salts in our custody?' I questioned hurriedly.

'Yes, sir.' the constable responded.

'Good, get a sachet of salt and bring it to me immediately.'

'Sir, that is evidence…' the constable protested.

'I said go and get it,' I shouted.

'Ok, sir. It is stored in a warehouse nearby. I will get it,' the constable saluted and left in a jiffy.

'Don't worry. I got what you want,' I said to Boris.

He nodded. He was trembling badly, and his legs were shaking.

'Ok, tell me one thing, what all did that lady ask you and since when?'

'The lady used to come there along with Mr. Allen. They would always come together. She would pluck the plants and seed a new one.'

'Oh. How much time would it take for the bulb to appear and for it to flower?' I asked.

'Around twelve weeks,' he said. Now he was shivering badly.

'So, every time the flower is ripe enough, Lakshmi Trust would pluck the entire plant.'

Boris nodded.

I took a mental note. It meant that the flower was required to keep on growing because its latex and flower juice could be used only when it is completely uprooted.

Furthermore, Lakshmi would do partial experiments only here, and she would work mostly on the plantation fields of Andrew Carlson.

The constable had arrived with a sachet of salt that we had seized on the boat a few days ago. I gave the sachet to Boris.

Boris opened it up haphazardly and put the content in his mouth. It gave him the satisfaction of life. His trembling stopped, and his sweating did too. He was feeling comfortable, and his face had a visible sense of satisfaction.

Boris was extremely addicted to drugs. Maybe Louis had caught him twenty-four hours ago, and that's why Boris did not have drugs for many hours, and his body was craving for it.

'Ok, you may go.'

'Thanks, you gave me this,' Boris said, showing the sachet.

'It is alright.'

'You can get the seeds of that plant in the basement of the bungalow if you are interested,' Boris said, getting up and leaving.

'No, I don't need the seeds,' I said. 'Wait a minute – you said basement.' I was shocked.

'Yes, sir.' Boris stood at the gate.

'There was a basement in Bungalow no. 9,' I asked surprisingly.

'Yes, sir.'

'Can you show me.'

'Yes, sir.'

I was shocked. I rushed immediately with Boris. My Vauxhall Astra was repaired to an extent, and I was happy to note that. I pushed Boris into my car, and we both immediately rushed to the bungalow.

I was at the bungalow– the Bungalow no. 9, and there were police constables and barricade tape. Boris and I went inside the bungalow. Boris led me to the staircase, and at the half-turn landing -where I had found the Alfa Combat - Boris jumped, holding onto the handrail.

He jumped once, twice, and thrice, and with the third jump, the wall in front gave way, revealing another staircase below. The wall just opposite the internal staircase had a hidden door to the basement – surprising. I looked at Borris Allen in complete dismay, as if was saying I couldn't figure that out.

We both descended the stairs and rushed to that open area, continuing down towards the basement. Boris guided me through the dark area and stairs which had a peculiar curve. Boris then pressed some button, and the place lit up.

It was a huge space, and I had not seen this place before. It seemed that when I arrived, the people inside were hiding here. Perhaps, one person was with Lisa, holding her at gunpoint or something. The basement was large and contained many seeds of Lakshmi plants, as Boris had mentioned. Additionally, there was a table and a chair, along with numerous envelopes and letters. These letters were from Sarah Taylor and were sent to different addresses. What did it mean? I checked the envelopes and a letter inside. It appeared that these were the customers or the drug dealers. I found one with Marianna's address as well. These people would then give money to Sarah Taylor, and she would indicate whom to supply the drugs to through these letters. The letters had different numbers of pages. It seemed to be a customer greeting page.

These letters were sent to this bungalow. Johnson Allen would come here occasionally, see these letters, and accordingly supply the drugs from his warehouse. This was a unique way to distribute drugs.

'Is there any exit from the basement directly outside?' I questioned.

'Yes,' Boris said.

He took me to the other side of the basement where there was another curved staircase. I followed Boris up the staircase. He reached the top and gave three punches, one after the other, and the floor slid aside. He got up and gestured for me to come up. We were near the place where the BMW e21 car was parked.

Now, I understood the entire game. These people were hiding here, and then they went to the other side and left in the BMW e21.

Boris was extremely helpful, looking at me with great expectation.

'Don't worry, I will give you two more sachets for this help,' I said.

Boris was elated and happy.

I was now in shock, and we returned to the police station. I kept thinking that day I should have seen this basement as well. I must have pushed the girl inside and arrested those people. Then I would have prevented two murders from happening.

I gave Boris two more sachets and asked him to leave. In the meantime, I didn't realise that Louis had come to the police station with Ms. Taylor.

There was a huge commotion outside the police station. Many media persons were asking why an innocent civilian, a housewife, and that too, of a missing police officer's wife, had been arrested. Louis wanted to handle the media; however, I indicated that I would take them on.

I went outside, and the media was ready with various questions. There was a loud buzzing sound of various reporters, cameras were on, and many seasoned journalists had gathered at the scene. The lane outside the police station was cramped due to the presence of so many people.

One of the reporters shouted, 'Is this how low the London police have stooped down? There are no arrests for the double murder in Bungalow no. 9, but an innocent civilian is arrested.'

'Let me state that Ms. Taylor has been arrested because we wanted to investigate this case from all angles,' I replied.

'Why arrest her? She would have cooperated,' another reporter stated.

'Well, I guess you don't doubt our actions. We know what we are doing,' I responded calmly.

'From your actions, it seems like a cover-up. A cop is missing, and you've arrested his wife,' another journalist said.

'Let me state that I am very close to solving this case. I know who the boss is – the hidden mastermind – the kingpin behind London Mafia.'

There was complete silence.

'If you have the mastermind – tell us now.' One of the journalists shouted.

'So that the mastermind can run away. Is that you want?' I countered.

'But...' the journalist started to retort, but I shouted before he could speak, 'If all of you can wait for just a couple of days, let me reassure you – you will see the end of the drug mafia. It's a story you would not believe – a puzzle unsolved till now.'

The journalists didn't know what to say. The police inspector was asking a short time.

'I will request you all to give me some time, and I will present to you the story of your life.' I concluded and got up to return.

I left and returned inside. The sound of journalists leaving one by one could be heard in the background.

Louis was there beside me. He asked, 'Why did you let that Boris Allen go?'

'He was useful. Thanks. But he was an extremely small fry. A victim of drugs himself.'

'What? I thought he was the murderer.'

'No, Louis. Have you not seen him? He was dull, lethargic, and non-violent.'

'I agree.'

'The crime was committed with brutal force. Smashing the heads of sexagenarian people. A crime like that was not something Boris Allen would do.'

'Ok. I thought since the property was to devolve on him....'

'No, Louis,' I cut him off. 'The property was not supposed to devolve to him. That Assistant Registrar played a trick.'

Louis was shocked to hear this.

'But I am glad you got this person. He was very helpful to our cause. I guess when the intent is right, even the Gods try to help us.'

Louis was still in shock and not entirely clear about what I wanted to convey. I left him and soon joined Ms. Taylor where she was being held. There were female constables, and Ms. Taylor appeared petrified.

'I know you are innocent,' I reassured her.

'Then...' She could hardly utter a word.

I gestured to the female constables and asked them to bring water.

'You want to meet Watson. Right?' I asked.

She nodded.

'Believe me, Watson himself will come to meet you now.'

She was shocked and didn't believe me. She looked into my eyes, and then she sighed.

I held her hands and stroked them gently. Even Louis and the constables were confused. I had arrested someone, but I was treating her as if she were a friend's wife. So why had I arrested her in the first place?

Alex also had come to the station. He inquired, 'Sir, what is the purpose of arresting...'

'To get to Watson,' I answered before Alex could complete his sentence.

'Okay. What's next?'

'We have to go to another address in Edinburgh.'

'Again, to Edinburgh.'

'Yes.'

'I'm ready.'

'Then let's go.'

Alex, while driving, said, 'I just don't understand one thing.'

'I can guess,' I said.

'What?' Alex said and stared at me.

I gestured for him to concentrate on the long road.

'You are worried about why we're going to Polwarth.'

'Yes.'

'Because Nicholas had said so.'

'But he had plainly lied. Why would he help us.'

'Tell me one thing, Alex.'

'Yes.'

'If you were Nicholas, what would you have done?'

'I would have run away from the hospital. I don't think he couldn't manage to run away.'

'Exactly. But he was there.'

'So what?'

'That means he had no place to go.'

'You said that he was sure that if he goes out in the open, the mafia would kill him,' Alex asked.

'Yes. Because the mafia was not yet aware Nicholas had been caught and was in the hospital. They would come to know eventually but as of now they are not aware. Now, if he runs and goes to his usual hideouts, the mafia would know about it soon and possibly kill him.'

'But how does it make sense to go to Polwarth.'

'Dear Alex, you are missing the point. Think as Nicholas.'

'I got it.'

'Good.'

'If I am Nicholas and I want to run from this hospital, I need to go to some place secure. But before I can go there, I need to ensure that those whom I fear are neutralised. The best option is to let the most feared cop – the great Richard Carlsen – go after that person.'

'Great, Alex.'

'Sir, you are exceptional. You can think of things that a normal mortal can't even dream.'

'Thanks, Alex. Now, speed up. We are a bit late.'

Alex drove the entire four hundred or so miles distance, covering the entire trip in around eight hours. In the past few days, we had travelled between London and Edinburgh twice, a remarkable amount of long-distance travel for my career. During this journey, I had time to make mental notes and connect the various dots that were scattered about. I was trying to piece together the complete story. In the midst of this, I realised that I hadn't informed Emily that I was heading to Scotland. It was a sudden decision.

'Alex, stop whenever you think it's convenient. I need to tell Emily that I am in Scotland,' I said.

'There is a petrol station nearby. I will stop there, and you can make the call,' Alex responded.

I contemplated for a moment and then changed my mind.

'Well, let's finish the meeting at Polwarth.' I said while lighting my Havan cigar.

'Why? Emily would be extremely worried.' Alex insisted.

'I know. Something is telling me that we should not stop before Polwarth. It's one of those premonitions. You continue,' I said authoritatively.

Alex nodded and continued at a brisk pace on that long highway. Soon, we arrived at Polwarth. It was almost midnight when we entered the area. The place was deserted. The one-storey building, which appeared devoid of human presence, stood tall. It was built on a plot of around two hundred and eighty square yards, I would guess. Alex and I were cautious, each holding our respective firearms in hand, ready for action.

We could see that the building had a small window. Both of us entered the building through that open window. It was dark, so I switched on my lighter, and we took measured steps. We entered a living room, and from there, we moved into another room that looked like a bedroom. I sensed a person sleeping on the bed, so we entered carefully, with Alex following me. We found a switchboard and turned on the light.

Alex shouted, 'Hands up!'

The person who was sleeping got up. He was shocked to see two police personnel at that hour in his bedroom. He was petrified and shaken. We could see he was a sexagenarian. We gestured for him to get up, and slowly he got up from his bed.

'Who else is there in the house? I shouted.

'No one.' The old man said it with bated breath.

I gestured to Alex, and soon he went into other rooms and switched on all the lights. It was a three-bedroom house with a living room and a kitchen.

'There ain't no one.' Alex said.

We took the old man to the living room and made him sit on the sofa comfortably. Alex got some water for him.

'I am Richard Carlsen, Senior Police Inspector, London Police.' I said.

'Ok.' replied the old man.

'May I know your name, please, sir?' I asked politely.

'Craig Smith.'

'Do you know any Nicholas?' I asked.

'No. I've never heard that name before.' The person replied.

I was not sure why Nicholas had given this address. Did he play us? It was a fake address.

'I hope Alexander has not done anything wrong again.' The old man replied.

'Alexander?' I asked, surprised.

The old man indicated in a photograph that was fixed there on the wall. It was him and Alexander. I got a shocker. Alexander looked like the same person as the second security guard, barring the facial scar.

'You are the father of Alexander?' I asked.

'Grandfather. His parents died when he was just fifteen.' The old man replied.

I took the photo frame and handed it over to Alex.

'You know that your grandson is working with the mafia?' I said it with intent and purpose.

'Officer, he was helping the poor child.'

'Poor child.' I questioned.

'Lisa.' The old man said

'Lisa, you mean Lisa Ross.' I said.

'Yes.'

'Daughter of Sam Ross?' I asked.

'Yes.'

'How does Alexander know Lisa Ross?'

'Both of them were in college together at the University of Edinburgh.'

'What?'

'Can you tell me where Alexander is?'

'I don't know; I met him about a week ago.'

'What did he say?'

'He said he was going to meet someone named Vijay at Allen Manufacturing. There was something big going on, involving drugs, and he said he had to help Lisa.'

'Was Lisa his girlfriend?' I asked.

'Well, at least a good friend, from what I know.'

'Is there any other close friend of theirs? Another boy,' I asked.

'I suppose you are talking about Stewart.'

'Stewart,' I exclaimed.

'Stewart was very close to Alexander and Lisa. He worked for Carlson Marine and Transport as a driver, driving their trucks. He wanted to make a lot of money and thus worked overtime.'

I looked at Alex, and he understood. The first security guard whom I met was Stewart, and the second was Alexander.

'Do you have any pictures of Stewart?' I asked.

'Yes,' the old man replied.

He got up and went to his bedroom, returning with an album containing many pictures of Lisa, Alexander, and Stewart having a good time together.

'Did anyone come to threaten Alexander?' I asked.

'Yes. Someone came a few days ago and threatened to kill me,' the old man said.

'What?' I exclaimed.

'Yes, he wanted Alexander to do something. I knew he was blackmailing him.'

'Can you describe that person?'

'He looked like a person of Indian descent,' the old man said.

'Vijay,' I said spontaneously.

'You rest here. Let me get that person for you. Don't worry, nothing will happen to Alexander,' I assured him.

Alex and I left the place with a picture of Alexander and Stewart from the album.

'Where to?' Alex asked.

'Allen Manufacturing,' I said.

'What will we get there?'

'I don't know. But if I'm not wrong, we might get the address of Vijay.'

'From where?'

'Do you remember Vijay showed us the administrative building? It might have records.'

'But won't they destroy it?'

'No. They don't know that we have Nicholas with us. They don't know we've met Craig Smith. They don't know that we will raid Allen Manufacturing.'

'And after our last satisfactory visit, they'll be a bit off guard.'

'Yes, and now they'll be thinking that we're investigating Ms. Taylor.'

'But you haven't told Emily. Don't you think she'll be worried?' Alex said, wondering why I hadn't informed Emily that it would take time. I had been away from home since morning, and it was now almost one o'clock at night.

'Yes, Alex. Let me call her. Stop near a telephone booth.'

I called home, and the phone rang, but no one answered. I checked my wristwatch; it was half past one in the morning. I dialled again, but there was no response. I couldn't understand why Emily wasn't at home. Where could she have gone at this late hour? Something didn't feel right.

'What happened? You look troubled,' Alex asked.

'Emily didn't answer the call,' I said.

'At this hour, she's not at home?' Alex exclaimed.

'I'm not sure. Let me call Melvin and ask him to check,' I said.

I returned to the phone booth and dialled Melvin's house number.

'Hello,' Melvin's half-awake voice answered.

'Melvin, I need a personal favour,' I said.

'Yes, sir,' Melvin replied immediately, his voice becoming more alert.

'Please go to my home and check whether Emily is alright,' I requested.

'Okay, sir.'

'I'll call my house again in about another hour or so. You be there,' I instructed.

'I will be, sir. Don't worry. My Ducati is the fastest,' he reassured me.

'Thank you,' I said and ended the call.

'Why do you think Emily may be in danger?' Alex asked, looking at my worried expression.

'I don't know, Alex. Watson could take Emily hostage to force me to leave Ms. Taylor.'

'What? Would Watson stoop that low?' Alex questioned; his tone filled with anger.

'I'm not sure.'

'Hmm.'

'Let's go to Allen Manufacturing,' I said.

We reached the facility, and to our surprise, there was no guard standing there. We sneaked through the outer gate and went straight to the administrative building. There was a room where the lights were on, and we could feel the presence of many people.

I and Alex were on our guard. We slowly moved with measured steps. We reached the entrance of the room, which was open, and we peeped inside. Both Alex and I were wondering who was there when a voice came from behind us.

'Drop your weapons, officers.'

I and Alex both could feel that some gun was pinching our backs. We dropped our guns and turned.

It was Henry Walter who was standing in front of us, along with Sarah Taylor, his daughter. He had two Alfa Combats in his hands. I and Alex were shocked. I was not that surprised knowing that he was alive; knowing I would see him here like this though was a big surprise.

He gestured, and we both started moving inside the room. We saw Vijay standing with another Alfa Combat in his hand, and Lisa Ross, Stewart, and Alexander were sitting on the chair. It seemed they had received a brutal beating. Lisa had no clothes on her body, and it meant she was exploited badly by Vijay and Henry Walter. Stewart and Alexander were also brutally beaten up.

Finally, I could see the dishevelled lady who had the guts to take on the mafia.

Henry Walter gestured, and I was made to sit on a chair, as was Alex. Sarah Taylor also came inside.

'The great Carlsen, finally we could meet. Did I surprise you? Henry Walter said

'No Walter. I knew you were the one who killed Andrew.'

'What?' Walter was surprised.

'I could deduce easily.' I said.

'You are a genius. You must work with us.' Henry said.

'Thanks for the offer, but I know your entire game now.' I said.

'Is it so? Then tell us.' Henry said it astonishingly. He had a certain pride in his statement. Henry was a well-built, middle-aged man. He was muscular and strong, and his bluish eyes made him look elegant. He was wearing a casual button-down Burberry shirt and Calvin Klein jeans. The Rolex date-adjust two tone was shimmering delightfully on his left hand. He was looking like a rich mafia lord who was in complete command of things.

'I will, Henry. But first, let these three innocent children go.' I said, pointing towards Lisa, Stewart, and Alexander.

'No.' growled Henry. 'They are not innocent. This bitch caused irreparable harm to me.'

'I know that. But still, I insist.'

'Haha.' Henry laughed loudly. 'You insist. I think you have not seen where you are. At my mercy.' Henry shouted.

'I can only request; the rest is up to you.' I said.

'Ok, let's do a deal. If you could tell me about what you've deduced, maybe I can consider letting your wish come true.'

I cleared my throat and got up from my seat. I took my police jacket and gave it to Lisa. She was now covered properly. I sat back in my seat. Henry Walter and Sarah exchanged looks, and both of them had hatred for Lisa and nothing else.

'It was simple, Henry. You and Watson were hands in gloves. Your daughter Sarah had told you that Lakshmi had made this great discovery. Even Lakshmi wanted to deal in drugs. She attempted it also but failed.'

'Wow, your start is good.' Henry said in between.

'It was at that time that Lisa met Lakshmi, and they met Sam Ross. Sam wanted to get into the business of drugs. He wanted to eliminate you completely. He committed a mistake and took the help of Andrew Carlson, who was a good friend of yours, and Johnson Allen. You and Watson made the plan and killed Sam.'

'Yes. I asked Andrew to let Sam come to the warehouse that day. I told Watson to conduct the raid. Watson came while I and Andrew held Sam, and then Watson killed him with a bullet. We dropped the huge acid on Sam. Sam had kept huge amounts of acid stored in warehouse as he wanted to use them for camouflaging drugs. It was such an apt death for him.' Henry Walter said in a straight voice. He had such a deep satisfaction saying that he had planned so well to kill his fiercest competition.

'You got the hint that police might know about Lakshmi Trust and her meeting you, so you ensured that Sam Ross died and it was believed that Henry Walter died. So that even that angle of drug getting camouflaged is not investigated further.' I continued.

'You are brilliant Carlsen.' Henry Walter exclaimed. He continued, 'Laxmi Trust got arrested while trying to sell camouflaged drugs and police got a hint of such a mischief. But with the news of my death this news died down. This was also one of the reasons why I wanted to show that Henry Walter died and not Sam Ross. Obviously, the other reason was to control the arms supply business.'

'You then declared yourself Sam Ross and usurped the Alfa Combat business also. You never worked directly but let the daughter Lisa be the middle person.' I continued.

'All was going well when this stupid brainless bitch decided to double-cross.' Henry growled and slapped her.

'But why, Lisa, was working with you when she knew that you were not Sam Ross?' I questioned.

'That is what you have to answer – the great Carlsen.'

'She never intended to work with you. She wanted to destroy you. Her working with you was just a ploy,' I said.

'Wow, you are brilliant.'

'She worked with you to know all the secrets, and then she wanted to exploit,' I said. I waited for a minute and then continued my monologue. 'The drama of Sarah and Lisa's fight was also to just mislead people into thinking that Sarah was disturbed.'

'You are good.' Henry Walter said.

'She worked one-year for you, and that's when she even introduced Alexander and Stewart, her two besties in the team. They all got to know your secrets. Everything. That's when they knew that Sarah was telling you the address by sending post. Lisa wanted to tell everything to the police. She told Forbes. You got the shock of your life.'

'Yes.'

'But you committed a mistake. Here, Johnson Allen and Andrew, they also grew greedy. Even Lakshmi wanted a larger slice. They knew that it was they only who could work this magic. It was at that time you decided to kill

Johnson Allen and Lakshmi Trust and put the blame on Lisa, Stewart, and Alexander. That's why they were called there.'

'Good lord. How could you guess so well?'

'He is Richard Carlsen, not a dumbass like you.' Alex intervened in between.

Henry hit Alex with the butt of his Alfa combat, and Alex cried in pain. His lips got cut by the fierce blow.

'You continue, great Carlsen,' Henry said.

'But before you wanted to kill them, you wanted to have a final negotiation. In that meantime, Lisa called me. Watson and I arrived there, and you got surprised. You had little time. You told Stewart and Alexander to play ball, else you would kill Lisa, and also you threatened to kill the grandpa of Alexander.'

'You know about Craig too. You are exceptional,' Henry said.

'Not only this, Sarah forced Alexander to give a contract for my killing to Nicholas and also to make changes in the Registry office so that if ever things went wrong, Alexander would get arrested.'

'Smart,' Henry said.

'You, after killing Johnson Allen and Lakshmi, hid in the basement, and from there, you ran away. I heard a yowl, but that was because you punched the door hard and hurt yourself while coming up from the ground. You, Lisa, Alexander, and Stewart, along with Watson, ran away from the surrogate tunnel, which opened at the parked car. You all sat and ran away. But somehow, Lisa managed to escape in the melee. You did not want to take chances, as I was around. You let Lisa go. Lisa then made a call to Forbes twice. Lisa understood that I was there to help you genuinely.'

'But we have got this dumb girl. You can see she had been treated nicely by me and Vijay.' Henry laughed, looking at her.

'I don't understand when Lisa was at loose how she again got in your grasp.'

'So, you – the great Carlsen – don't have all the answers. Good, so I don't have to honour my words,' Henry peevishly said.

'Henry.' I shouted.

'This stupid girl...' Henry walked towards Lisa and pulled the jacket I had given her. Lisa was totally naked, and that distracted the attention of both Henry and Vijay. It gave Alex and me just that split second, and that was enough. I pounced upon Henry, and Alex on Vijay.

I landed a Karate chop on Henry's nape. Henry cried in pain. His Alfa Combat dropped. Alex also with a swift action twisted Vijay's arm and made him drop his gun. Before Henry or Vijay could do anything or call their stooges, Alex fired at Vijay's both legs' knee cap. Vijay cried in extreme pain. I also did the same with Henry. I fired at the two legs, and the knee caps were shattered. Henry was in extreme pain.

Henry committed a mistake of not doing the same with us when he had both me and Alex in captivity. Our training was that in such cases, never waste time in side talks but neutralise the enemy asap. The gunshots attracted a few of the goons, but Henry and Vijay both were lying on the ground bleeding, and we had the guns pointed at their heads. That was enough to give cold shivers to all of them.

Sarah was in shock. She had never seen such brutal police officers who never thought twice before shooting. Sarah wanted to run away, but Alex fired at her leg. She cried in pain.

Henry shouted, 'No... Sarah my child.'

Alex hit Henry as brutally as he could. Henry could not understand how things have changed in a jiffy. He underestimated both me and Alex. What he did not know was that we were extremely good in close quarter battles.

Before anyone could understand anything, Alex fired another shot at Vijay's thighs. Alex growled, 'One wrong step, and Henry, Vijay, and Sarah all will be dead.'

Vijay was in extreme pain and bleeding profusely. If he was not given medical treatment in a short time, he would definitely die a painful death. Henry had seen the devil in Alex. He did not want to take a chance. Someone who, without provocation, can shoot bullets in their legs could do anything if provoked.

'Henry, if you don't want to die, ask your stooges to arrange for a car,' I shouted.

Henry gestured to one of his persons.

I got Henry and Sarah, as well as Lisa, in one car. Both Henry and Sarah were bleeding profusely. Alex got Vijay, Alexander, and Stewart in his own Astra. Soon, we reached the Edinburgh Hospital, and we got Henry, Vijay, and Sarah admitted.

I called Forbes from the hospital, and surprisingly, even at that hour, Forbes picked up the call. He was aware that such a thing could happen.

'Sir, I have got Henry Walter arrested,' I said.

'Henry Walter,' Forbes said, shocked to hear that.

'Yes. It is a long story. But right now, I have called because I need help.'

'I could have fathomed that. When you said you want to go alone, I have told my friend in Scotland. Where are you?' Forbes said in an assuring tone.

'Sir, in the Edinburgh Central Hospital. Need backup.'

'It is reaching in fifteen minutes. Just hold the fort till then,' Forbes said and cut the call.

I could feel the sense of pride in his tone. He was happy that I had done this all alone. Forbes always had admired me as I get the results. Soon, a contingent of Scotland police came, and they took over.

Lisa – the dishevelled lady – hugged me extremely tightly. I also hugged her hard. I then gestured Alex to drop Alexander and Stewart at their home. Alex left.

I then went to call my home. It was more than an hour. Melvin would be waiting for my call. I dialled, and the call was answered. I almost fainted hearing the voice from the other side.

'You wanted your wife?' Watson shouted over the phone.

'Watson?' I said, shocked. 'What are you doing in my home? Where are Emily and Melvin?'

'Melvin is dead.' Watson said in a dry stoic voice.

'Noo...' It was shocking news for me. Melvin was a young vibrant boy. 'Watson, I will kill you if something happens to Emily!' I shouted in a fierce tone.

'You come here as fast as you can. Bring my wife. Give happiness, take happiness,' Watson shouted and cut the call.

I was shocked. Watson killed Melvin. What had happened to him? I could never imagine Watson like this. Was Watson the real kingpin?

I dialled Louis. He answered the call as usual in one ring even at this hour.

'Louis, Melvin is dead. Watson had killed him, and now Watson has kept Emily at gunpoint,' I said before Louis could have asked anything.

'What?' Louis was shocked.

'I need your help.'

'I will send a force to your house,' Louis responded.

'No!' I shouted.

'Ok, Sir. What do you want from me?' Louis said.

'I will handle Watson alone. That is my personal fight. But I am in Edinburgh. Can you ensure that no one leaves from my house till I arrive.'

'Ok, Sir. Let me arrange something.'

'Thanks, Louis,' I said politely and cut the call.

Alex had come to the hospital by then. I told him everything and asked him to be careful. Though now the Scotland Yard was there, Alex was still required to explain the situation. I rushed to my car and saw Lisa standing at the hospital gate. She was in the police jacket I had given her. I waved to her to say goodbye.

'Please take me with you.' Lisa pleaded.

I was not sure why she wanted to come with me, but I could understand her state of mind. At this hour, she had no place to go. She was also a prime witness, and it was my duty to protect her.

'Ok. Hop in.' I said, waving my hand.

Soon I was rushing towards London. It was a long, long journey, almost eight to nine hours, and I knew that Watson would hold on to Emily, even for an old friendship.

'Are you alright?' I asked Lisa.

'Yes.'

'I am sorry you have to go through this.'

'I am ok, Richard. In fact, I am happy that you are such an exceptional detective. I made a mistake by not relying on you that day.'

'I am sorry,' I said, surprisingly.

'You were right. After the death of my father, I joined Henry Walter. He also needed me because he wanted to capture the arms market as well. Sam Ross' loyalist wouldn't support him if he had declared that he had killed Sam Ross. Thus, he used me, I was the one you was handling the arms business. Walter, with the help of Ross's name and sending me to do the deals, slowly captured the drugs and arms mafia. I was with him until I learned the secrets. Johnson Allen, Lakshmi, and Andrew, they were all with Walter. They were making lots of money. I slowly gathered proof. I made Alexander and Stewart part of the team. When I learned enough, I sent a report to Forbes and told him about the trucks.'

'But didn't Walter come to know it was you?'

'No. The only mistake I made was with Watson.'

'But when you were with Henry for so long, you should have known that Watson was his man.'

'I knew that, but someone made me believe that Watson was a double agent. He was a police guy acting to be with Walter like I.'

'Oh. That's why you met Watson.'

'Yes. I told Watson that Johnson Allen and Lakshmi were planning to double-cross Walter. Watson, instead of helping me, took me, Alexander, and Stewart to Bungalow no. 9. The plan was simple; kill Johnson Allen and Lakshmi, blame it on Alexander and Stewart. I was not sure what they had planned for me.'

'But then you called me, I came ...'

'The person who made me believe that Watson was a double agent was so close to you that I thought you and Watson are together in this, and I did not allow you in. I was at gunpoint anyway.'

'Understood.'

'And who was this close person of mine?'

Chapter XI

THE ENDGAME

I didn't realise when I had reached my home. It was almost dusk on that Sunday evening. I entered my house as it was open, Smith & Wesson 10 in hand, ready to fire.

'You can relax, my friend,' I heard a familiar voice.

I could see Watson inside my bedroom. I went in that direction.

'You came without my wife,' Watson growled.

I could see Emily sitting on a chair.

'Where is Melvin?' I shouted.

'I told you,' Watson said.

He gestured with his hand, and I opened the door of the next room. I could see the lifeless body of Melvin. It filled me with immense grief.

'How could you, Watson?' I shouted.

'The police had failed me. The mafia hailed me,' Watson answered, showing no remorse for killing a fellow policeman.

'Emily,' I shouted. 'Are you okay?'

'As of now,' Watson replied.

'What do you want?' I asked.

'Simple, bring my wife. I said give and take,' Watson said.

'And...'

'Nothing. I will leave with my wife.'

'What about Emily?'

'She is your wife, I promise I won't do any harm to her.'

'Let me call the police station.'

'But no over-smartness. You know I am a sharpshooter. Emily's life is just a trigger press away,' Watson said peevishly.

Emily was sitting in the chair, appearing exhausted by the turn of events. She had witnessed the death of a fellow police officer at the hands of another close friend. She must have been terrified.

I dialled the police station. Louis answered the call. I said,

'Louis, is Ms. Taylor safe in custody?'

'Yes, sir.'

Watson was looking at me, gesturing to hurry up.

'Louis, I need urgent, or let me say, very urgent help.'

'Yes, sir.'

Watson was apparently getting bored, and he gestured to hurry up.

'Please bring the force. I have got Watson covered,' I shouted.

'What the...' Watson said and aimed to shoot me.

However, before he could shoot, I fired. I was ready, and Watson didn't see it coming. The shot hit his stomach, and he began to bleed, falling to the ground.

Emily rushed toward me, shocked.

Lisa Ross was coming from behind me, and I gestured for Emily to stay away with my Smith & Wesson. I gestured for her to get in the room.

Watson was bleeding, and I picked up his gun and gave it to Lisa Ross.

'If Emily moves a bit, don't flinch, shoot1' I shouted.

'Richard,' Emily was flabbergasted.

'If she utters a word, shoot,' I said to Lisa.

Emily was shocked. She never expected such behaviour from her beloved husband.

I shoved Watson into the room where Melvin's lifeless body lay.

'My friend, you can enjoy the company of your erstwhile colleague until I speak to my good wife!' I shouted and shut the door closed.

Emily sat in the chair, and Lisa and I entered the room. Both of us had weapons in our hands.

'Lisa, you know Emily – my wife.'

'Richard, are you out of your mind?' Emily said.

'Why, Emily?' I asked.

'What are you doing? Will you listen to this daughter of the mafia or to me?' Emily said.

'How do you know she is the daughter of the mafia?' I questioned.

Emily remained silent.

'Emily, it was such a pain to know about your true self. I started crying badly.'

'Richard, let me explain, please,' Emily said softly.

'Why, Emily?' I was lost in emotions.

And I didn't realise that Emily was extremely quick. In that moment of frailty, I just lost it for a second, and that was enough for Emily. She jumped with the agility of a cheetah and hit me with a well-executed karate chop. I fell to the ground, and she picked up my gun and hit Lisa with the butt of that pistol. Lisa fell on the bed, and Emily took her pistol too.

In a matter of seconds, Emily had taken our pistols, and before we could realise, she fired two shots – one at each of me and Lisa. I cried in pain. The bullet pierced my thighs, and Lisa's kneecap was shattered. We were in extreme pain. Before Lisa and I could even understand further, Emily fired another shot at me, and my other thigh was struck by a bullet as well. She knew no mercy, and in a matter of seconds, I was profusely bleeding.

I was more in emotional pain than physical. Emily had made both me and Lisa immobile in a matter of seconds.

'You wanted to know why?' Emily growled. 'Right, Richard.'

I looked at her with teary eyes.

'You stupid cop. You never realised who was the kingpin. It was me. I was the lord of London mafia all the time. Henry Walter and Sam Ross, these two were my stooges. They would do what I said.'

'Our love ___' I tried to say.

'What love, you stupid idiot?' Emily shouted. 'I had the cover of a crime journalist. But the problem was that cover could be blown anytime. Forbes got a whiff. I was under watch. Then I met you. I thought being a housewife would be the perfect cover. I married you. The best part was you were always busy, and thus I could manage the show.'

'That's why you kept for digging information.' I said.

'Yes. That was icing on the cake. Now I could even know what the police were doing.'

I looked at her with hatred.

'It was then when I saw Watson was dejected, and I asked Walter to offer Watson a role. Watson obliged. That was the time when this girl's father,' Emily said, pressing her hand onto Lisa's knee. Lisa cried out in immense pain.

I could also feel Lisa's pain. Emily continued, 'That stupid Sam Ross wanted to be greater than me. He discovered a drug that could be camouflaged as powdered sugar. He told that to Andrew. I knew that Sam Ross could cheat. He did. He tried to sell some drugs, but that failed because even Lakshmi was learning the tricks at that time.'

I was in pain, and Emily kicked me at my wound. I cried out.

'Listen carefully, you dumbo!' Emily shouted.

'At that time, I made the plan. I killed Sam Ross. I asked Henry Walter to be Sam Ross. I asked Lisa to be the middleman. All was going well, but Lisa turned out to be a traitor.'

'Did she know about you earlier?' I asked.

Emily kicked my wound again, and I cried out in pain.

'Stupid Carlsen, no one knew about me except Sam Ross and Henry Walter.'

'Lisa called Forbes, and the truck got arrested by Alex. I could guess what these stupid people can't. So, I asked Henry Walter to tell Watson to meet Lisa. Watson met Lisa and told her that he wanted to destroy the gang. He was working with Walter at the insistence of the famous Richard Carlsen.'

'What?' I said.

'Yes. Lisa then came to your house just to cross-check when she met me. She did not know about me. But it was famous everywhere that I know whatever Richard knows. I called Watson and introduced him to Lisa. I confirmed to Lisa that Watson was working against the interest of Walter. Lisa was fooled too.'

Emily took a break. She glanced at Lisa who also in pain.

'Though Lisa was constantly at the lookout for the mysterious kingpin, and to befool her I kept the consumed cigar butt of yours in bungalow so that she could be made believe that Forbes the police commissioner was the one who was visiting that bungalow.'

Lisa was looking Emily with extreme hatred.

'But Lisa was sharp and to confirm she wanted to have a look at the diary which Sam Ross used to keep. That diary would be the only proof where he had in his own writing written about me. Lisa came to know that her father - Sam Ross's diary was in the locker of Bungalow no.9. I only knew how to open that locker, no one else. She first tried to force open that locker, but when she couldn't succeed she simply called the police station for help.'

'I thought that police force would come. But when only you and Watson came, I got confused. More so, everyone knew that you consumed that special cigar whose butt I had seen in the bungalow. So, I thought you were with them and thus did not let you in. But I didn't realize that I actually was helping these criminals by not allowing you in.' Lisa said. She was in excruciating pain.

'But what did you get from this, Emily?' I was not interested in those minute details that transpired that day. I was dejected and heart-broken.

'Stupid Richard. I am the king of this city. The arms and drugs this city needs, I supply. You know how powerful I am?'

'But now your game is over.'

'Stupid Richard. Nothing is over. I will kill both of you and blame it on Watson. I will let Watson die also. You shot at him. Henry Walter might be saved by now. You think that Alex alone could manage the show that long.'

'Emily!' I shouted.

'Richard. I love you.' Emily aimed my head and was about to fire.

Bang!

A shot was fired, and Emily was lying on the ground. Louis had arrived in time and shot Emily in the leg. Before Emily could react, Louis and the police team captured her.

I hugged Louis.

'I can't thank you enough,' I said.

'It is my duty,' Louis said.

I indicated that Watson was in the next room.

I limped and reached the phone. I immediately dialled Forbes. I was worried about Alex.

'Hello,' Forbes answered the call.

'Is Alex safe?' I questioned. I didn't want Alex to be bothered either by the police or by the mafia.

'Yes, Richard. Scotland Yard has reached and taken Henry Walter and Vijay into custody. They have recorded Alex's statement too. Alex is safe and sound. How about you? How is Emily?'

'Sir, long story. I will tell you later. But thanks again,' I said and hung up.

I was almost fainting because of the blood loss, pain, and the emotional trauma of discovering that the love of my life was not what she seemed but a cruel game of destiny.

I fainted, and when I woke up, I was in the hospital.

Now, almost three months have passed since that bloody Sunday in October 1982. Emily, the mafia king pin – the closest person to me - was being prosecuted. The diary of Sam Ross was recovered from the locker of Bungalow no.9 and it had many details that helped with many details of Emily. Watson had recovered and was now in jail. Henry Walter, Sarah Walter, and Vijay as well. Lisa Ross had recovered and had disappeared. She had always been the mysterious girl who started this story with a mysterious call, which ended up ruining my life completely.

I lost a dear friend, lost the love of my life, lost a colleague and this trauma impacted me for life. I never knew that the end of this story would be so cruel. The London Mafia was temporarily finished, but with it, so was the fabled Richard Carlsen. I would not recover from the fact that my wife – the love of my life – would be taken away from me by destiny like this. This was my story, my bane.

THE END

Aalekh Award given by Bennett University – Times of India Group, to this maiden attempt by Namit Shastry.

Award given away by celebrated leaders and authors Dr. Kiran Bedi (IPS) and Dr. Ramesh Pokhriyal Nishank – ex CM Uttarakhand.

www.ingramcontent.com/pod-product-compliance
Lightning Source LLC
LaVergne TN
LVHW041024150826
845672LV00001B/190